THE AFTER EDEN SERIES

TEK-FALL

(METAL FLESH and HELL'S MENAGERIE)

AUSTIN DRAGON

Published by Well-Tailored Books, California

Tek-Fall / The After Eden Series

978-0-9967060-4-9 (hardcover)
978-0-9967060-3-2 (paperback)

http://www.austindragon.com

Book cover design by Leslie K.
Formatting by Polgarus Studio

Printed in the United States of America

*"After Eden, Thy Kingdom Fall.
All Kingdoms Fall, New Kingdoms Rise."*

World War III. It was inevitably going to be one of religion, this great, grim, evil war of humans, machines, and *other things* in the shadows that have never existed before. Unfortunately, neither the cause nor the outcome was within our perception, though the former should have been. No one could ever have imagined that it would not just be the third of the world wars, as that is unremarkable, but the explosion of the first global war of the Technological Age, the Tek Age—a hell we had never seen before.

"With the benefit of more than fifty years since the end of direct American involvement in the pre-Caliphate Middle East, we can see in stark detail that despite the miraculous advancements in medical tek and forever-changing gear, the human soldier has remained virtually the same after several thousands of years. I fear we may have already arrived at the 'NHA Battlefield'—no humans allowed—as future wars will showcase such an array of biologically destructive machines and weapon systems that no normal human soldier will be able to survive, for even a moment. Any future 'manned' wars will be fought with surrogate robots and cybernetically advanced or genetically engineered super soldiers." – Colonel "Tiny" Garrison, MD, PhD, M.I.T Military Academy, 2079

"Such is the dual state of modern man—coldly god-like and amorally child-like. It is not a new scientific theory in sociocultural anthropology. The more civilization advances technologically, the more humankind regresses and de-evolves. 'Humanity' itself fades and dies away; then the world…falls. This eventuality is called Tek-Fall." – Mister Alpha (real name disputed), believed to be one of the Founders of the pre-Magi Order, circa 2050

Net-Dictionary

Wolf 359

1. A red dwarf star located in the Leo constellation, approximately 7.8 light-years from Earth, making it one of the stars nearest to our solar system.

2. A fictional space battle in the Star Trek Universe between the United Federation of Planets and the Borg Collective in the year 2367.

3. The opening battle of World War III in New York City on September 11, 2125. Over sixty percent of the United States of America Atlantic Oceanic Battle Fleet was destroyed by the Supreme Islamic Caliphate Battle Group on the first day.

Other terms:

Pagan: (universal or American usage) a non-believer of god or gods; one that doesn't believe in religion, often negative to, hostile to, or hateful of religion.

Jew-Christian: (American usage [by non-religious people]) a religious person, other than Muslim.

Faither: (global usage [by religious people]) a religious person, other than Muslim.

Tek World: common slang for tek-cities, tek-metropolises, or general tek-society.

Resistance: (pre-World War III)

1. [by non-religious people] government term for the network of Jew-Christian domestic "terrorists" in America.

2. [by religious people] the civilian resistance force against the militant, anti-religious American government.

Continuum:

1. (general usage) the parallel society created by and controlled exclusively by Faithers outside of Tek World.

2. (formal usage) the formal alliance of the New Protestant Order, New Jewish Continuum, New Catholic Order, Mormon Order, the African Collective, Shogun, and the Magi.

Table of Contents

METAL FLESH

THE AFTER EDEN SERIES: TEK-FALL
EPISODE I

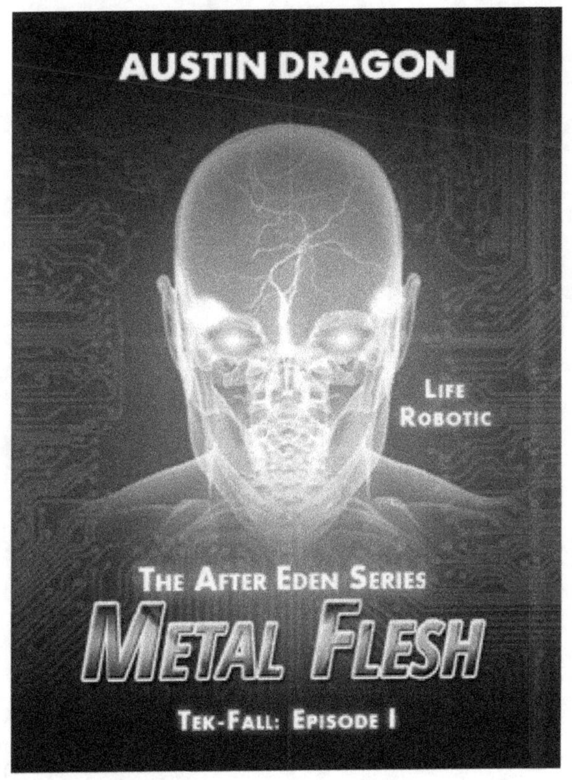

The Metal Flesh Poem

God creates Man.
Man rejects God.
Man creates Machines.
Machines become God.
Man accepts new God.
Machines kill Man.
Machines self-terminate.
God resets the universe.

The following story takes place *after* the events of

Thy Kingdom Fall (After Eden Series, Book #1)

during the events of

Stars and Scorpions (After Eden Series, Book #2)

and *before* the events of

Rising Leviathan (After Eden Series, Book #3)

Chapter One: Sprocket

I must find the Jew-Christian called Goth Lila.

The thought quickly fades from his mind as a figure ambles into his line of sight. It lurches forward from the shadows. At first a tall, lanky silhouette, then fully visible—a bald humanoid robot of bright silver construction, with glowing red digital eyes and infested with…worms. Large pink worms wiggle from every metallic pore and every crevice of its robotic body. It stops in front of him, its head swivels to face him, and it sticks out a grayish tongue at him. It smiles, then continues its walk through the bustling human crowds of the tek-city.

Sprocket watches, sitting on the bare pavement on the corner—the same spot he has barely moved from in almost four days. The hallucinations are growing more frequent. Supposedly, by next week he will be unable to distinguish between reality and dreams. The body must sleep, it must dream, and if you don't let it, it will do so without your permission, and with your eyes wide open. He has been awake for three days straight, but well within "safe" levels.

Dayton, Ohio is a tek-city like all others. Environmentally, it is never too hot, never too cold. The hidden air regulators, built into every building, keep all that "unkind" weather of the natural world away from the population. No one living here—most have never been anywhere else, other than to travel from one tek-city to another via enclosed transportation—knows what it is to feel a natural cool breeze, a winter draft, summer humidity, or a drop of a snowflake on the skin. Rain is the only element they've experienced, and that is tolerated by the Grid only for urban sanitation reasons—"Let's give the tek-city a good shower." The average Jew-Christian would probably say, "That's like a muddy pig taking a bath in a pool of mud." He knows about real weather because he has ventured and even lived in the territories outside the tek-cities—the retro-tek Outlands and the dangerous Trog-lands.

He pops another "zombie" into his mouth. The *stimulagenic* gum has been his only companion these past days. He must stay awake on what is hopefully the end of his endless stakeout. The good news is that zombies allow you to stay awake seemingly forever, if you want. The bad news is that the longer you use them, hallucinations and daymares start to occur. Then the insanity creeps in, reversible at first, and then the irreversible psychosis stage arrives. He has another week at least before that happens, but he must risk it. It's the very moment he closes his eyes that she'll turn up. That's what happened three times before. He's been tracking her up and down the coast and across the country for years now.

Sprocket is grungier than usual, dressed in black skin-jeans, a thick t-shirt, and covered by a thin, transparent leather hoodie. He doesn't like hair on his face, but he forgot his palm-shaver so, just as he hates, he has a mustache and the beginnings of a beard that look like someone drew them on with a makeup marker. His long dark brown hair is disheveled, except for a casual part to keep it out of his dark brown eyes.

He hears laughter and glances up to see a surveillance globe-drone with big, red lips and big, white teeth hovering fifteen feet in the air. Government surveillance drones are everywhere watching the people, twenty-inch-diameter flying spheres in a muted silver color. But there are many more commercial drones—flying digital billboards, flashing people with their rapid stop-motion live-def static photos or full-fledged vids. Neither type of drone has lips and teeth. Visual *and* auditory hallucinations now—not good.

It's really not accurate to say, "If you've seen one, you've seen them all." Every tek-city has some bit of uniqueness. The Northwest has more trees, while the East loves its vertical construction, with taller residential and commercial towers than other parts of the country. The Midwest is more into horizontal construction, sprawling the tek-city over wider stretches of land. But to most people, they're all the same. The ever-flashing, ever-changing, noisy digital billboards sit on top of commercial buildings—as if the commercial drones weren't enough—with advertisements (advids) of music, movies, clothes, the latest devices, the latest cars, restaurants, vacations, sex, and drugs. There is no such thing as a dimly lit or quiet tek-city.

For tek-city dwellers, the fashion styles are endless. There are traditional business types in their office suits, shirts, maybe vests, maybe ties, maybe not, in a variety of colors from simple blacks and whites to earth tones to natural rainbow colors to synthetic, techno colors, or even the so-called futuristic shiny silver everything. Then the traditional faux-leather, plastic, cloth, or hemp dress shoes or trendy glow-boots or -shoes. On the other end of the spectrum would be the nudist or quasi-nudist, but there aren't many in major tek-cities. They stay mostly in the Outlands and Trog-land. From time to time, you see one of them, totally nude or wearing a single piece of clothing. There is even a hard-core group called Streakers who run around naked, yelling at everyone wherever they go, wearing only five-toe slip-on sandals. Though nudity is legal, most people avoid it because of sexual germs, harsh drug vapor, and all the micro-chemicals the tek-cities spray into the air for population health maintenance.

In between, you have casuals like Sprocket. The style is never an office suit of any kind, but rather skin-jeans, skinny jeans, straight-cut jeans, bell-bottom jeans, or bucket jeans, of any solid color or assorted mix. Casual shirts, tee shirts, sleeveless tops, half-tops—any color, any pattern, with words or symbols or not. Also, a wide variety of glow clothes. Hats galore are common, from simple to outrageous. If it were sunny, there would be people with day umbrellas.

But it's not the clothes that make the "people of the future." It's the "toys." It's their ubiquitous devices: playing-card-sized e-pads, eight-by-eleven-inch tablets (each, usually with a handle or case), ear-sets (a combination phone, headset and ear bud worn in one ear or both, or attached to glasses), and even wearable tek, the merging of device and clothing. Most people also wear clear glasses, used for visual interface—text floating at the sides of your field of view: the current time, the name of a caller, the number of voice messages or emails, a dot indicating breaking news stories, etc. The glasses can be programmed to display anything.

With all this chatter, it looks like everyone is talking to themselves. "Tek-chatting" is the term for the universal way of multi-tasking—talking on the phone, walking somewhere, working on your mobile devices, getting lunch, walking the robo-pet. All these people together in a crowd and not one of them talking to the person next to them, all talking to someone they're not seeing face to face, or, more likely, their own home computer assistant. Every person is a separate unit doing his or her own singular thing.

"Beautiful people" is what his bio-dad used to call them. A world of no poverty, no hunger, every disease and ailment genetically or surgically erased, and none of the "human refuse" of the Outlands and Trog-land—Nihilists, Anarchists, Drug Zombies, and the like. Tek World is utopia—isn't it?

A furry ball scurries across the sidewalk right under his legs. *Was that a robo-mouse?* He's seen them in the Outlands, created by tek-punks with too much free time on their hands, but they would never be allowed here in a major tek-city. *It must be another hallucination.* All his hallucinations seem to have a mechanical component to them. He doesn't know why.

Sprocket imagines that this is exactly what his bio-dad used to do—people-watching, his favorite pastime. He thinks about his bio-dad often. New Atlantic City, New Jersey, 4 January 2089 was the last time he saw his "Daddio" alive—his biological father, ex-cop, famous journalist, Logan. He helped him track down a source for a story. That was four years ago—it's 2093 now, seven years from the supposed great twenty-second century. Isn't every century better than the previous one and all of human history before? Logan had a lot of friends in law enforcement, but none of them helped. His father's case—"death by unnatural causes"—was closed two years ago. But it was *how* they closed the case. One day his police friends were obsessed with finding out what had happened to Logan. Then, they were all "unavailable" for any direct communication. He got an official email from District HQ that the case was closed and that was that. But it was not the end for Sprocket. He has been on his own private quest ever since.

There they are! Three Goths are walking down the street, dressed in their typical all-black Goth gear. They must be Jew-Christians. It is the nuance of their dress that is the giveaway—if you know what to look for.

He remembers the conversation with his bio-dad, the last day he would ever see him.

"Daddio, I'm not finished. Goths wear their black clothes, black tattoos, black piercings, but not all of them are Nihilists, Hedonists, or Zombies. Did you know some of them are JCs?"

Logan is surprised. "Really?" If a Jew-Christian wanted to hide in the general population, that would be a good way to do it. "Hiding in plain sight."

"And Trogs."

Trog is the common slang for those who hate tek—they avoid not only using it, but even being near it. For the average tek-dweller, it's a state of being, so alien, so deranged, so inhuman. People cannot live without the mechanization of the Tek World.

"But Trogs hate tek. That's why they're called Trogs."

"Daddio, two kinds of Trogs—those who hate tek and those who hate tek controlled by the government but are very much tek-heads. If you don't have any contacts, find a JC Goth to get you to a JC tek-head Trog, and they'll get you a JC tek-lord."

Sprocket is distracted again by something next to him—his bio-dad Logan is sitting on the ground, smiling at him, in exactly the same pose. *Stop! Daddio is not here!*

Gender-specific terms like "mother" and "father" were banned many years ago and new terms like "bio-mom" and "bio-dad" are frowned upon in the anti-religious, pan-sexual, politically correct majority society of Tek World. "Parent" and "guardian" are the acceptable terms, but Sprocket is all about rejecting conventional wisdom. The fact that there are six genders in Tek World doesn't change the fact that his bio-dad was a male, not a she-he, he-she, hermaphrodite, or neut (genetically asexual person). Like any proper young person worth any value, non-conformity is the only way to be.

Now I'm having discussions with myself! He snaps his head back to look across the street. The Goths are gone! The hallucination of his father was not real. *Were the Goths fake too?*

Sprocket jumps up and runs across the street. A car screeches to a halt, knocking him to the ground. The front passenger-side window lowers.

"What's wrong with you?" the passenger yells. "We got the whole thing on vid-cam, you dumb, stupid idiot, so don't even think of filing an insurance claim against us or trying to sue us."

"Yeah, we got you recorded, dumb, stupid idiot," another man's voice says from inside the car.

Sprocket ignores them and picks himself up, but he almost falls back down. He's been sitting so long that his legs are asleep. *There's that laughing again.* He looks up and the man looking at him is now a translucent-skinned clown robot with fiery red hair and three glowing digital eyes. On top of the car about a dozen giggling three-inch stick robots dance, each knocking their butt against another.

"Sprocket, you need to sleep," the man/clown says. "Why don't you lie down where you are and forget about Logan? Yes, that's it."

Sprocket is confused. "But I'm standing. Why did you say that?—'Yes, that's it.'" Suddenly, he's lying on the street. There is no man/clown, car, or dancing pixy robots. People are looking at him. Sprocket slowly stands. He looks at the spot across the street again.

Were the JCs real or not?

Cars drive themselves in a tek-city. You sit back, tell it where to go, and it takes you there. Auto-drive—with the driver-less smart-car tek of vid-cams, collision-avoidance laser-sonar, GPS sat-link, and Grid traffic management—ended vehicular fatalities forever in a nation of six hundred million people. He jaywalks across the street to the spot where he last saw them and looks around.

Is that them?

Sprocket sees one of the Goths at the end of the street, waiting and his back to him. He starts walking toward the Goth through the crowded sidewalk. A man bumps into him.

"Sorry," Sprocket instinctively says.

The man says nothing, but watches him. Sprocket continues to walk, but stares back at the man. The man is a Muslim. Sprocket can tell by his left armband, which is adorned with a crescent symbol. Islam is still the only paleo-religion not scared to proudly and clearly identify its religiosity; no one else dares. Jews and Christians live beyond Trog-land or hide in the tek-cities. American Hindus and Sikhs left for CHIN (Chinese-Indian Alliance) territory years ago. Even neo-religions like Vampires, Vulcans, Jedis, Arthurians, and Foundationalists feel more comfortable in the Outlands. Sprocket has made himself into a kind of religious expert over the past few years.

There is something off about this man. Sprocket continues to stare at him. The man angrily stares back.

"Why are you staring at me?" the man yells.

"I'm walking this way. You didn't plant some kind of bomb or something down here, did you?"

"That is outrageous slander against me! Muslims are not terrorists! You are the terrorist!"

Terrorism still happens—Trog-land Anarchists mostly and the rare "rogue" Muslim.

"I just don't want anything to blow up in my face because that will be a big, big red light in my book."

"You are the terrorist!"

"Then why were you staring at me like you did something you weren't supposed to do?"

"You were staring at me."

"No, I wasn't."

"Yes, you were."

"You were staring at me, Johnnie-o."

"I was staring at you because you were in my way and trying to walk through the wall."

Sprocket slaps himself hard in the face and forcibly shakes his head. He opens his eyes and sees a silver wall inches from his nose. He looks to the left. The man he was talking to is no longer there, only the normal crowds of people going about their business. He looks to the right. At the end of the street the Goth is still there with his back facing him.

"We've been followed by the best operators in the business, but you are truly the most pathetic we've seen," a voice says.

Sprocket turns around to see four large Goths surrounding him.

"It took you one hour just to cross the street," a Goth says. "And then you tried walking through a wall."

A skinny, grinning, half-naked kid appears next to them. "Suck in those fumes," he says and points up. Plumes are four-foot high poles of various styles, weighted to the ground, that release a steady flow of psychogenic, hallucinogenic, or stimulagenic drug vapors for the public to "sample."

One of the Goths kicks the kid in the stomach.

"Oww!" the kid yells as he doubles over. He is wearing only shiny, silver briefs and slippers. "What did you do that for?"

"Were we talking to you?" a Goth asks.

"I was talking to you," the kid says.

Sprocket starts to laugh, a little at first, then uncontrollably. He looks up to notice a swarm of drones above him, watching with human eyes.

"*He's dream-trancing again.*" Sprocket hears the voice. It is the voice of one of the Goths surrounding him, but none of them are talking to him. The voice sounds like it's from someplace else. He feels funny.

"Hello," Sprocket says. "Who's talking to me?"

"You know who's talking to you."

"I'm standing on the street with four Goths around me and they're talking to this kid—"

"You're not on the street. You're not even in the tek-city anymore. You're in a van. Can't you see my face?" the voice says.

Sprocket starts to panic. "Help me. I can't tell what's real. This isn't supposed to happen for another week, before the bad side-effects start. I was going to stop days before that happened."

"Who told you that? How many of these zombies have you taken? How many days? You're in psychosis now, you Drug Zombie."

"I'm not a Drug Zombie."

"Says the man overdosing in front of us. We don't know who you are, but we're going to dump you on the side of the road. No one would be dumb enough to hire the likes of you for any surveillance and tailing job."

"No, don't dump me. I need to find someone. Her name is Goth Lila."

There is silence. Or there is silence in the world he can't see.

Sprocket's fear grows as he watches the dream-world in front of him. Hallucinations can't hurt him, no matter how strange or disturbing. But is that true?

"Are you still there?" Sprocket yells.

"How do you know her?" the voice says.

The Goths, the kid, the crowds of people are all androids with glowing eyes and start breaking apart.

"I know Goths. I know of her."

The buildings around him start to disintegrate and collapse to dust.

"How would any Pagan know that?"

He jumps, startled as the moon itself crashes to the ground with unimaginable force. The entire ground starts to burst apart in front of him.

"I got skills. I don't care, religious or not. I travel in whatever circles I need to for my business. I'm a businessman. She's the one I know can help me find some people. I've been tracking her for three years, and I'm not stopping until I get those answers. The only chance I had to catch up to you this time was to do something that you wouldn't do—not sleep. I'm going to get those answers, even if it kills me."

"What day is it?"

"Why?"

"How many days have you been taking zombies?"

"I've been up for four days, but only using them the last two days."

"What date did you start taking them? What day do you think it is?"

"I know what day it is." *The earth starts to break up and he is floating in space. Other planets converge to crash into the sun.* "It's the afternoon. It's 8 January 2093."

"Well, Mr. Sprocket, you may have done just that."

"What? Did what?"

"Killed yourself. You've been taking the zombies for two weeks!"

Science Division, Washington, DC
7:57 a.m., 3 January 2093

The underground offices are spacious white rooms, spotless white like all other areas of the facilities. The scientist in his white lab coat leads the two men wearing black suits to the lounge area. They sit in empty bubble chairs and the scientist touches a button on the arm of his chair to activate the privacy screen. A blue light turns on above them, no external sounds can get in and their conversation cannot be heard.

"Sorry, but my normal office is doing some highly confidential work," the scientist says.

"We understand," says one of the men. "We did come unannounced. May I ask you something very simple?"

"Yes, please do."

"Do wormholes really exist?"

The scientist thinks, 'How odd a question.' He says, "I'll assume you mean the ones in theoretical space physics and not the ones you find in the dirt outside, made by the common earthworm. Yes, they do."

"Could someone…theoretically…travel through one?"

The scientist smiles. "Are you being serious?"

"Yes, we are."

"No, that is science fiction, sir. Everything people think they know about them is not real. You can't create a spaceship to fly through one to another point in the universe, or another dimension, or another time. The only thing science fiction has gotten right about them is that they are unstable. A wormhole could be the size of a pinhole, and no one has proven that they can even exist in a planetary atmosphere."

"Are you sure?"

"Well, yes. Until some scientist comes along and proves us all wrong, like Galileo came along and proved to the scientific community that the Earth was not flat at all."

"Would you be interested in being part of a special team that the President's science director is putting together?"

"For what exactly?"

"Please be advised what we're talking about now is highly classified top-secret and cannot be disclosed to anyone outside this room."

The other man in black takes a portable privacy screen device from his jacket, sets it on the arm of his chair, and activates it.

"Sir, I've held the highest security clearances for a better part of thirty years."

The lead man continues. "Yes, we know, sir."

"This special team would be to do what exactly?"

"To determine if there is any possibility that a secret...a terrorist organization may have located a terrestrial wormhole and is planning to use it as a weapon against the United States of America or another nation."

"Sir, that's not possible. A wormhole can't be a...weapon."

"Would you join our special science team then? The science director wants to ensure that it isn't a possibility."

Secret Underground Location
7:52 p.m., 8 January 2093

The hallway of the secret headquarters is filled with armed Goths. The freight elevator opens and more exit. The arriving group greets the others with handshakes and hugs. Mikel, of the Goth Jews, is led to the main rooms.

The room looks like an oversize, multi-colored hotel suite in direct contrast to the singular appearance and dress of the Goths in nothing but black. Goths collectively aren't a religious Order, but are made up of separate and distinct groups—some friendly to each other, some hostile to each other, and others completely indifferent to each other. Only a small percentage is religious, and they are very much aligned.

There are many kinds of Goths: Hedonists, Nihilists,

Anarchists, Vampires, Wiccans, Witches, and Faithers. Gothism is more than black hair, black makeup, and black leather clothes; it is an attitude. However, no one who is not a Goth knows what that means. A Goth Christian can instantly spot a Goth Hedonist, and a Goth Anarchist can recognize a Goth Jew on sight. For those outside Gothism, all Goths look alike. Both Goth Jews and Goth Christians are the main human intelligence gatherers in Tek World for Faithers.

Mikel continues his briefing. "The Mormons have moved out their last city-ship to the Russian-Asiatic territory."

Five Goths sit at the conference table. Goth Christian Lila sits across from him. She has three piercings in each ear lobe, and wears black eyeliner and three ring necklaces. On the ceiling, the yellow light of their privacy screen is on.

"All your people will be gone too soon," she says.

Mikel nods. "Yes. Your people will be the Continuum's last eyes and ears on the ground here."

"How is it over there?"

"The Russian Bloc and Asian Consortium are okay. We've always maintained ties there."

"You have Russian ancestry, don't you?"

"On my grandmother's side." He paused to think. "We'll have to become new Goths. Black is a minority color over there, especially in the Russian Bloc. It's bright reds, yellows, blues, greens, purples, or silver-whites for hair color over there."

Goth Lila laughs. "You'll be the new Rainbow Goth Order then."

"We will. I'm a natural redhead, you know."

"Oh Mikel, why didn't you tell me all this before I got married."

They laugh.

"Where will you be based?" she asks.

"Africa." Mikel taps his palm tablet and an image of Sprocket appears on the screen. "What about him?"

"He will come in handy."

"Who is he?" Mikel asks.

"A low-level, independent grifter. His name is Sprocket, and his father was the one who Goli was helping back in '89 on an investigation. The Continuum got a ton of intel from it."

Goli is one of the best teks in the Continuum, a giant of a man, and a member of the Conservative Jewish Order. His specialty is hacking into Grids of countries (especially America) without the government's ability to track him.

"The President's killing of his own national campaign manager."

"A campaign manager aptly named Lucifer, but who cares. One killed the other before the other could strike first. It's always nice to see our enemies destroying each other—less work for us. We actually know this Sprocket. He's moved in some of the same circles as my people for many years. They killed his father too. His name was Logan. Goli flagged the case because the death was unusual and undetermined."

"You know full well that this Sprocket has undoubtedly been tagged by the government."

Lila smiles and says, "He wouldn't be any use to us if he weren't."

Chapter Two: Goth Lila

**Executive Branch, Non-Public Off-Site Offices,
Washington, DC
8:00 a.m., 9 January 2093**

Mahogany benches line dimly lit, underground hallways of marble floors and antique stucco walls and ceilings. This may be one of the most powerful tek-cities in the world, but it's still the District and here, historical preservation and construction reminiscent of the past is the norm—by law. People stream through these offices around the clock.

A large meeting room is filled with men and women in dark suits, except for a man dressed in gray, who walks from the door to the front of the gathering. They are all employees of the Homeland Defense and Intelligence Agency, the most powerful agency in America.

"Good morning, ladies, gentlemen, and all genders." He glances at his e-pad. "It looks like everyone is here and on time. Thank you. I will skip introductions since we have all had the pleasure of knowing and working with each other for years. I am here to officially announce that all outer-tek-city counter-terrorism interdiction operations are suspended until further notice. The memo is already being circulated to your offices."

People look at each other, surprised. Many are not happy.

"Sir, may we ask who the new directive is from?" a woman asks.

"Straight from Homeland herself and the President."

"Sir," begins a blond-haired man, "we are honestly going to suspend *all* interdiction operations? The President put them in place to protect the country. He did so before he was even President."

"Yes, I know. I was there too. And now he's issued a new directive for us to follow. Presidents can do that, you know."

"Yes sir, but may we have more detail?"

"The talks that have been ongoing in secret to hold a world summit of the superpowers may actually be happening."

Some are surprised; others stifle laughs or shake their heads.

"So we're really going to have a Federation?" a man asks, half-laughing.

"We're the humans," says another man. "The Muslims and CHINs are the aliens," says another.

"May we all get back to the meeting," the man in gray says. "The President wants Homeland to concentrate on de-escalating the tensions with the outer-tek-city territories—"

"Sir," the blond man interrupts. "These are not outer-tek-city territories. These areas are hotbeds of terrorists, anarchists, and subversives."

"And how have we been doing in the last decade? Be honest. It's just us in the room."

"Sir, that is not a fair question because ever since the use of direct action was suspended, we've been operating with one hand behind our back. If the President allowed us to take off the gloves—"

The man in gray interrupts, "The Russian Bloc touts every day that it is the true planetary utopia, where its religious and normal people live in perfect harmony. Then it shows America on their media, of course, using images from decades ago of riots, protests, and demonstrations. Since it looks like this summit will happen, the President doesn't want any of those images on the media anymore.

"This doesn't mean that Homeland will not be fighting terrorism or monitoring suspects. It simply means that we will not be leaving the tek-city to go into their territory. People want to live outside the tek-cities, fine. We will be ceasing their immediate access. People will have to apply for passes to enter the cities from the Outlands and the Trog territories."

The crowd nods in approval.

"They can't cause trouble if they can't get into the tek-city."

"Which means they will just fester outside our walls," the blond man says.

"What would you do? What would 'taking the gloves off' mean?"

"Enable tactical drone strikes without the need for three-party confirmation."

"One-party only? That's been rejected by the Supreme Senate on more than one occasion. All strikes must also be approved by the Supreme Senate leader and the state's governor. It's a dead issue, so why keep bringing it up? What else you have?"

"We should completely end all access to the tek-cities from the outer regions."

"So it should be illegal to live outside a tek-city?"

"Yes."

"I don't think that would go anywhere politically or legally since we have more than a few governors, senators, and congresspeople who live in their own palatial mini-enclaves outside the tek-cities on both land and sea. So it's definitely not Trog civil rights lawyers that are the problem."

"Sir, all of us in this room know what the threat is, and pretending it's not there, for political reasons, doesn't make it go away. I say we make it go away before we have one or more serious attacks on the people, and they make our jobs go away."

The man in gray smirks. "I don't think we need to worry about the unemployment line yet. Thank you for the analysis, though."

"You're welcome, sir."

"Ladies, gentlemen, and all genders, any other questions?"

"What about current interdiction operations, sir?" a man asks.

"How many do we have?"

The man looks at his secure palm-tablet. "Computer, current live Operation Pinprick numbers?" He looks up. "Sir, we have over two hundred thousand live."

"Cancel the ones that haven't launched yet and allow the others to proceed. After that, all teams will be re-tasked. Any other questions?"

"Media, sir?" a woman asks.

"As far as the outside media, nothing is different. This is internal and confidential—for our eyes only." He holds up his hands. "Everyone, listen to me closely. This is not a retreat by the President for political optics. We haven't given up the strategy. Every one of us is as committed and dedicated to the safety of the American people as anyone, more than the American people themselves. We're only changing our tactics. The President believes that this issue is beneath human beings. People should be doing the bigger things. We have our old-style drone defense and newer sim-drones. He wants us to have a new robot police force directly tasked to deal with the outer-tek territories. Let the Jew-Christians and Anarchists kill as many as they can because they aren't human and all we have to do is make more. We can make them faster than they can kill them."

"Self-replication has been approved then, sir?" the blond man asks.

"It has."

Pennsylvania
8:01 a.m., 9 January 2093

The vast, desert-like plains between the "Wild, Wild West" Trog-land and the territory of the Faithers looks barren. For as far as the eye can see, there is nothing but minimal wildlife.

A pack of feral dogs hides in the shadows between two mounds of dirt. They can hear it and they can feel it—the ground shakes a bit as the distant vehicle approaches. Their eyes sparkle; the internal optics of each drone adjusts to account for the distance and speed of the oncoming vehicle. They rise as a unit and scatter to take their positions. Drones can be made to look like anything, and when they are made to look indistinguishable from organic life, they are called sims.

They are not in their positions for long. The sim-drones are sucked into the ground all at once. If they were real dogs, they wouldn't have even had time to scream. The vehicle appears and passes by in a flash, traveling at well over two hundred miles an hour. First stop: Trog-land. Final destination: West Virginia.

Florida
8:09 a.m., 9 January 2093

The Homeland monitoring station is many miles away. The drone "population" is not controlled by people. With millions in service, it's not possible, and the A.I. of the Grid is far more efficient. The only exception to protocol is when high-value targets are involved.

"We lost them, sir," says the government agent sitting at his station.

"All of them?"

"Yes, sir. As usual."

"Were they able to capture a photo of the vehicle?"

"No sir, and once the drone is down, they automatically change course, so any trajectory projection is useless. We've used sim-drones that look like canines, rabbits, birds, snakes, frogs—anything. Insect ones can't even get past their electro-screens. These 'new model' sim-drones seem to be as useless as the older models. We have to send in people."

"Are you volunteering, agent?" His boss is not expecting an answer. He continues. "As of today, we don't have to worry about it anymore. We're being re-tasked; orders from Homeland herself. Shut everything down. One day we will build a robot that can circumvent their defenses. Government has infinite patience."

Pennsylvania
8:51 a.m., 9 January 2093

The bullet vehicle looks like a three-car fast-track (train) but with hover tek to drive across any terrain at speeds greater than three hundred miles an hour. The vessel's cockpit control has two drivers, each wearing clear glasses. They are watching the road and every other indicator and sensor from the vessel's main computer. On one side behind them, three men watch over the jamming, sensors, and communications stations. On the other side, three men oversee the weapons stations.

In the adjacent passenger car, Goth Lila sits reading a small, physical book. The only change in her clothing is that she is wearing a heavy faux-leather jacket and thick combat boots.

"Ground thumpers got seven sim-drones at the cactus junction," a male Goth says as he enters the section and sits across from her.

"They keep trying, so at least we know they still do 'love' us," Goth Lila says.

"I wonder how many tek-dwellers know that all their birds and pigeons are sim-drones?"

"Would it matter? They wouldn't do anything about it. Aren't pigeons birds?"

"No, they're rats."

"That's no way to talk about one of God's creatures."

"But didn't the Pagans tell you? Real birds are 'environmentally dirty' to the environment." They half-laugh. "When do we get out of this damn place?" he asks. "The Goth Jews are already out of the country."

"We're as important as everyone else is to the Project. We just have to finish our tasks."

He sighs. "I just want to get my family out of here."

"It'll arrive sooner than you think. Can you learn all those languages that fast?"

"I'm good. You told me so. What's this mission?"

Providence Enclave, Pennsylvania (Seven Days Earlier) 12:01 a.m., 2 January 2093

One of the founders of the Resistance Movement, the late Elder Mother Esther, once said, "Can the flapping of a butterfly cause a hurricane? Can the seizing of a book kill a nation?" The government Religion Registration Initiatives turned ordinary citizens into anti-government "freedom" fighters and permanently split the nation into two Americas. Religious leaders became quasi-military leaders before they knew it. Some embraced this fact;

others rejected it and disappeared into the tek-cities.

One of those Resistance leaders, "General" Moses Atticus, not only helped direct the Movement to its current path, less focused on being "anti-government," but created a thriving Faith World. With the intra-civil wars in both American Christianity and Judaism brought to a final end, their sole existence could not only be about opposing the Grid government of the current President, who would most likely be in office for life.

Goth Lila was there when the Protestant Christian denominations of the Resistance met that fateful day—ex-members of dozens of denominations, from Anglican to Southern Baptist. A meeting of all the Resistance leaders from across the country, all thirty states—no Faithers lived in the other twenty-three American states. Today, there are Faithers probably in only twenty of the fifty-three States.

All the old Orders merged into the New Protestant Order, and the Resistance became the Continuum. Today, the full Continuum is not only the New Protestant Order, but the new unified Jewish Orders, the Mormon Order, the African Collective, the Shogun, and the Magi.

Goth Lila is allowed into the large, open conference room by guards as the official first meeting of the year is ending. On the holo-walls are the faces of other attendees at locations within the United States and far outside the country. One of the faces is that of "General" Moses. The images degrade to billions of flashing green dots and then the vid-screens go dark.

Within moments, the Continuum members start vacating the meeting room. General Moses' wife—equally respected and followed by the Faither community—is also in the room. Her name is Emma, formally called "Mother Moses," but simply known by all as "M."

Strategic meetings are formal and planned months in advance. But the frequent tactical meetings are smaller and occur whenever and wherever they can pull everyone together. Their tactical street intel meeting begins immediately in the corner of the room; half are Goths. M joins them and gives Lila a shoulder hug from the side. All the preliminaries of the meeting have already been handled. Tactical teams never meet long; most times, they are held to physically exchange tek or quickly debrief. Palm tablets with the new protocols are passed out to everyone. The devices are disposals, and as soon as the information is reviewed and transferred, they will be physically destroyed.

"As of today, Goth Lila is point," Mikel says "We'll all be at our new African base."

"Enjoy your *vacation*, Mikel," says one of men.

Mikel laughs. "I'll be sure to send you the postcards."

As the group disperses, M turns to Lila. "I hope you know how much the Continuum and all its members appreciate you."

"I'm just doing my job like everyone else."

"Your group was far more disjointed at the start, before you took charge. We want you to know that your hard work is noticed. Noticed and appreciated. And I'd be remiss in my religious duties if I didn't also add that you are loved and blessed."

Goth Lila can't help but smile. "Thank you, M. I'm not good at compliments."

"I know. Your mission is as important as everyone else's. It's subtle, but will benefit the entire Continuum and all its people long after all of our separate missions are over. It's by no means a trivial thing. All your people must know that."

Goth Lila nods. "They know."

"Also, my husband is sorry he can't grant your request. He promised this Mr. Edison Blair that he would never use his in-country contacts to reach out to him again. You must find others."

"I understand. A promise is important."

"However, Moses has no doubt in your ability to track down anyone you set your sights on."

"When I do find him, does anyone want him for anything else?"

"No, but we are very interested. It was a loose thread from the '80s and we like to close the books on any loose threads. Did you talk to Goli already?"

"I did. He said to be very careful."

"Yes, the contractor who killed this boy's father is codenamed 'The Man Made Out of String.' Considering how the man died and that his home's security was fully active, I don't especially like that codename. Moses talked to this Edison Blair. He warned Logan to take his investigation seriously; he didn't and now he's dead."

"But this time we're the hunters."

"Maybe, but never underestimate your prey. That's why the Continuum is so good. Our enemies always underestimate us, but we never reciprocate. You have a mission to complete."

"Do you miss it yourself, going out on street missions?"

M smiles. "Every day."

Charleston, West Virginia
2:07 p.m., 9 January 2093

A fast-track speeds by on the elevated mono-rail at one hundred fifty miles an hour. It's a twenty-car bullet train painted in a camouflage design of greens, browns, and off-whites. The busy expressway is to its right with queues of ten cars each, one after another, bumper to bumper in auto-drive mode driving at nearly ninety-five miles an hour.

Like many New England states, West Virginia has a large population of expatriates from former Western Europe after it fell to the Islamic Caliphate in 2065. In the Virginias, there is an over-representation of expat British, so much so that this region is often called Neo-Britain or the NUK (Neo-United Kingdom). Other than English, a few other languages are heard among the passengers—talking on their mobile devices.

A young female passenger is slumped in her chair, her head resting against the window. She's dressed completely in white—top, jacket, dress, and boots. Even her short hair is white. Everyone in this section can see that she's in distress. The man sitting next to her cautiously stands, seeing the beads of sweat on her forehead, and sits in another seat.

It is rare, but sometimes a storm trooper policeman or two rides the line. Two of them enter the compartment from the back of the train. Their uniform is a light, motorcycle-type helmet with a clear eye shield and navy-colored, full body-armor. The body-armor is bulletproof, explosion-resistant, fully linked to the Net for enhanced power, and equipped with internal surveillance using all optics and audios, a complete interface with the Grid to coordinate tactical operations, internal climate control, a GPS link, and exo-skeleton strength enhancements.

One of the passengers sees them and points to the woman.

"Hello, Miss," says one of the policemen.

The woman doesn't respond until he repeats himself another two times. She seems weak, but manages to sit up. Her eyes are squinting so she covers them with dark glasses.

"Are you okay, Miss? Are you sick?"

"I'm not feeling well."

"How long have you been feeling this way?"

"It started when I got back home."

"From where?"

"I was out of the country…in the Asian Consortium. In Thailand, I think. I shouldn't have eaten that food. I should never have eaten that real meat. Don't eat anything but pure, synthetic meat." She seems to doze off.

"Miss, I'm going to swipe your skin with a swab." The policeman reaches over and a small applicator extends from his index finger. He swipes it across her hand and wrist. It retracts and he lifts up the palm display of his glove to his face.

Three seconds later, the policeman steps back and his visor goes from clear to black as the lower half of the faceplate wraps around the rest of his face. His partner activates the same on his helmet.

"Miss, please come with us. We have to call CDC." Passengers closest to them start to jump up from their seats. "Everyone just remain calm and stay in your seats. Miss, can you hear me?"

"What?" she asks. She looks up at them. "What's happening?"

"You're sick, but we've already called for help."

She starts to stand. "Okay…but my portfolio…I need to…"

"Don't worry about that, Miss. We'll get it for you." He turns to his partner. "We'll have to quarantine the whole train until we know who she has had contact with."

"No," the woman says. "I can't be kept here. I have to get…to my destination." She almost falls back, but is grabbed by the policeman.

"Just have a seat, Miss. We'll have medics waiting for you."

His partner taps him on the arm. The portfolio is open and they look at what's inside—reams of diagrams, maps, and formulas on sheets of digital paper marked "Top-Secret" in red. There are also pictures, but the one that catches their eyes shows some kind of light beam blowing up the moon.

"What are these documents, Miss?"

"No!" The woman jumps up, startling everyone. She grabs at the documents.

One policeman pushes her back as the other grabs her wrists. They handcuff her and set her back down on the seat. The policemen stand back as she fights to get out of the handcuffs. Every passenger, from the closest to those at the end of the car, is standing and watching.

The policemen pay her no attention. She can struggle until the next Ice Age; she'll never get out.

"Terminate!" she yells at the documents.

Smoke! The portfolio is crackling and the police open it again. The data on the digital paper sheets is erasing.

"Record," one of the policemen says to his helmet computer. The data is gone and the sheets catch on fire. The policemen throw the portfolio to the ground. One of them grabs a white-water cylinder from his holster and fires it to put out the flames.

The woman has passed out from all her struggling with the handcuffs.

The fast-track arrives on time at the station, but all the passengers are kept aboard as Centers for Disease Control personnel go car-to-car to verify that each person is free of any contaminants. Plenty of uniformed police are on the scene, along with drones in the air and media trying to get a story. The woman is strapped and shackled to a hover-gurney by government medics in bio-suits.

"She's not contagious, whatever it is," one medic says to another.

The medics gesture as a third one backs up the ambulance to them. The arresting policemen approach them.

"How much of those documents did you record?" asks one policeman.

"Hopefully enough for the teks to reconstruct it." The policemen reach the medics. "Make sure she's not left alone," the policeman says to them. "In fact, we'll follow." He gestures to his partner.

"Officer, the woman is already dead," the medic says.

The policemen stop in place. "Is this a biological?" asks one of them.

"No, no. Not any kind of bio-terrorist attack. Whatever the contagion is, it is food-related, drug-related, or a mix."

"We need her identified—now," the other policeman says.

"We'll get you data as soon as we know. She's not in our registry, so she must be a foreign citizen."

The medics get the woman into the back of their ambulance. They secure the hover-gurney and close the door. *A minute passes, and the woman opens her eyes.*

Two medics get into the ambulance. As they drive out of the metro station, they look at the dashboard's rear compartment vid-screen and see the dead woman in the back. Ambulances are one of the only authorized vehicles, besides government police, that can bypass auto-drive.

The vehicle turns a corner and they hear something.

"What was that? Was that the door?"

They look at the vid-screen and it's dark. The driver slams on the brakes. The medics jump out and run to the back. The doors open. *It's empty.*

"Wasn't she dead?"

"We're in so much trouble."

The panicking medics backtrack on foot, looking all around as the Grid slows surrounding traffic to a stop.

Goth Lila has already taken off her white wig. She pulls off her facial mask. It takes her a minute to unpin her hair, shake it loose, and touch the buttons on her clothes—white turns to black.

The medics will look in vain. The police will review all surveillance from any Eyes or drone fly-bys in vain. She didn't jump out the back of the vehicle; it was her little android—and it flew out. She escaped the vehicle *before* the ambulance left. She leans back in the middle seats. There are two men, in the driver and passenger seats. The SUV continues to drive—they are already miles away.

Chapter Three: The Amish

**Executive Branch, Non-Public Off-Site Offices,
Washington, DC
8:00 a.m., 9 January 2093**

Mahogany benches line dimly lit, underground hallways of marble floors and antique stucco walls and ceilings. This may be one of the most powerful tek-cities in the world, but it's still the District and here, historical preservation and construction reminiscent of the past is the norm—by law. People stream through these offices around the clock.

A large meeting room is filled with men and women in dark suits, except for a man dressed in gray, who walks from the door to the front of the gathering. They are all employees of the Homeland Defense and Intelligence Agency, the most powerful agency in America.

"Good morning, ladies, gentlemen, and all genders." He glances at his e-pad. "It looks like everyone is here and on time. Thank you. I will skip introductions since we have all had the pleasure of knowing and working with each other for years. I am here to officially announce that all outer-tek-city counter-terrorism interdiction operations are suspended until further notice. The memo is already being circulated to your offices."

People look at each other, surprised. Many are not happy.

"Sir, may we ask who the new directive is from?" a woman asks.

"Straight from Homeland herself and the President."

"Sir," begins a blond-haired man, "we are honestly going to suspend *all* interdiction operations? The President put them in place to protect the country. He did so before he was even President."

"Yes, I know. I was there too. And now he's issued a new directive for us to follow. Presidents can do that, you know."

"Yes sir, but may we have more detail?"

"The talks that have been ongoing in secret to hold a world summit of the superpowers may actually be happening."

Some are surprised; others stifle laughs or shake their heads.

"So we're really going to have a Federation?" a man asks, half-laughing.

"We're the humans," says another man. "The Muslims and CHINs are the aliens," says another.

"May we all get back to the meeting," the man in gray says. "The President wants Homeland to concentrate on de-escalating the tensions with the outer-tek-city territories—"

"Sir," the blond man interrupts. "These are not outer-tek-city territories. These areas are hotbeds of terrorists, anarchists, and subversives."

"And how have we been doing in the last decade? Be honest. It's just us in the room."

"Sir, that is not a fair question because ever since the use of direct action was suspended, we've been operating with one hand behind our back. If the President allowed us to take off the gloves—"

The man in gray interrupts, "The Russian Bloc touts every day that it is the true planetary utopia, where its religious and normal people live in perfect harmony. Then it shows America on their media, of course, using images from decades ago of riots, protests, and demonstrations. Since it looks like this summit will happen, the President doesn't want any of those images on the media anymore.

"This doesn't mean that Homeland will not be fighting terrorism or monitoring suspects. It simply means that we will not be leaving the tek-city to go into their territory. People want to live outside the tek-cities, fine. We will be ceasing their immediate access. People will have to apply for passes to enter the cities from the Outlands and the Trog territories."

The crowd nods in approval.

"They can't cause trouble if they can't get into the tek-city."

"Which means they will just fester outside our walls," the blond man says.

"What would you do? What would 'taking the gloves off' mean?"

"Enable tactical drone strikes without the need for three-party confirmation."

"One-party only? That's been rejected by the Supreme Senate on more than one occasion. All strikes must also be approved by the Supreme Senate leader and the state's governor. It's a dead issue, so why keep bringing it up? What else you have?"

"We should completely end all access to the tek-cities from the outer regions."

"So it should be illegal to live outside a tek-city?"

"Yes."

"I don't think that would go anywhere politically or legally since we have more than a few governors, senators, and congresspeople who live in their own palatial mini-enclaves outside the tek-cities on both land and sea. So it's definitely not Trog civil rights lawyers that are the problem."

"Sir, all of us in this room know what the threat is, and pretending it's not there, for political reasons, doesn't make it go away. I say we make it go away before we have one or more serious attacks on the people, and they make our jobs go away."

The man in gray smirks. "I don't think we need to worry about the unemployment line yet. Thank you for the analysis, though."

"You're welcome, sir."

"Ladies, gentlemen, and all genders, any other questions?"

"What about current interdiction operations, sir?" a man asks.

"How many do we have?"

The man looks at his secure palm-tablet. "Computer, current live Operation Pinprick numbers?" He looks up. "Sir, we have over two hundred thousand live."

"Cancel the ones that haven't launched yet and allow the others to proceed. After that, all teams will be re-tasked. Any other questions?"

"Media, sir?" a woman asks.

"As far as the outside media, nothing is different. This is internal and confidential—for our eyes only." He holds up his hands. "Everyone, listen to me closely. This is not a retreat by the President for political optics. We haven't given up the strategy. Every one of us is as committed and dedicated to the safety of the American people as anyone, more than the American people themselves. We're only changing our tactics. The President believes that this issue is beneath human beings. People should be doing the bigger things. We have our old-style drone defense and newer sim-drones. He wants us to have a new robot police force directly tasked to deal with the outer-tek territories. Let the Jew-Christians and Anarchists kill as many as they can because they aren't human and all we have to do is make more. We can make them faster than they can kill them."

"Self-replication has been approved then, sir?" the blond man asks.

"It has."

Pennsylvania
8:01 a.m., 9 January 2093

The vast, desert-like plains between the "Wild, Wild West" Trog-land and the territory of the Faithers looks barren. For as far as the eye can see, there is nothing but minimal wildlife.

A pack of feral dogs hides in the shadows between two mounds of dirt. They can hear it and they can feel it—the ground shakes a bit as the distant vehicle approaches. Their eyes sparkle; the internal optics of each drone adjusts to account for the distance and speed of the oncoming vehicle. They rise as a unit and scatter to take their positions. Drones can be made to look like anything, and when they are made to look indistinguishable from organic life, they are called sims.

They are not in their positions for long. The sim-drones are sucked into the ground all at once. If they were real dogs, they wouldn't have even had time to scream. The vehicle appears and passes by in a flash, traveling at well over two hundred miles an hour. First stop: Trog-land. Final destination: West Virginia.

Florida
8:09 a.m., 9 January 2093

The Homeland monitoring station is many miles away. The drone "population" is not controlled by people. With millions in service, it's not possible, and the A.I. of the Grid is far more efficient. The only exception to protocol is when high-value targets are involved.

"We lost them, sir," says the government agent sitting at his station.

"All of them?"

"Yes, sir. As usual."

"Were they able to capture a photo of the vehicle?"

"No sir, and once the drone is down, they automatically change course, so any trajectory projection is useless. We've used sim-drones that look like canines, rabbits, birds, snakes, frogs—anything. Insect ones can't even get past their electro-screens. These 'new model' sim-drones seem to be as useless as the older models. We have to send in people."

"Are you volunteering, agent?" His boss is not expecting an answer. He continues. "As of today, we don't have to worry about it anymore. We're being re-tasked; orders from Homeland herself. Shut everything down. One day we will build a robot that can circumvent their defenses. Government has infinite patience."

Pennsylvania
8:51 a.m., 9 January 2093

The bullet vehicle looks like a three-car fast-track (train) but with hover tek to drive across any terrain at speeds greater than three hundred miles an hour. The vessel's cockpit control has two drivers, each wearing clear glasses. They are watching the road and every other indicator and sensor from the vessel's main computer. On one side behind them, three men watch over the jamming, sensors, and communications stations. On the other side, three men oversee the weapons stations.

In the adjacent passenger car, Goth Lila sits reading a small, physical book. The only change in her clothing is that she is wearing a heavy faux-leather jacket and thick combat boots.

"Ground thumpers got seven sim-drones at the cactus junction," a male Goth says as he enters the section and sits across from her.

"They keep trying, so at least we know they still do 'love' us," Goth Lila says.

"I wonder how many tek-dwellers know that all their birds and pigeons are sim-drones?"

"Would it matter? They wouldn't do anything about it. Aren't pigeons birds?"

"No, they're rats."

"That's no way to talk about one of God's creatures."

"But didn't the Pagans tell you? Real birds are 'environmentally dirty' to the environment." They half-laugh. "When do we get out of this damn place?" he asks. "The Goth Jews are already out of the country."

"We're as important as everyone else is to the Project. We just have to finish our tasks."

He sighs. "I just want to get my family out of here."

"It'll arrive sooner than you think. Can you learn all those languages that fast?"

"I'm good. You told me so. What's this mission?"

Providence Enclave, Pennsylvania (Seven Days Earlier) 12:01 a.m., 2 January 2093

One of the founders of the Resistance Movement, the late Elder Mother Esther, once said, "Can the flapping of a butterfly cause a hurricane? Can the seizing of a book kill a nation?" The government Religion Registration Initiatives turned ordinary citizens into anti-government "freedom" fighters and permanently split the nation into two Americas. Religious leaders became quasi-military leaders before they knew it. Some embraced this fact;

others rejected it and disappeared into the tek-cities.

One of those Resistance leaders, "General" Moses Atticus, not only helped direct the Movement to its current path, less focused on being "anti-government," but created a thriving Faith World. With the intra-civil wars in both American Christianity and Judaism brought to a final end, their sole existence could not only be about opposing the Grid government of the current President, who would most likely be in office for life.

Goth Lila was there when the Protestant Christian denominations of the Resistance met that fateful day—ex-members of dozens of denominations, from Anglican to Southern Baptist. A meeting of all the Resistance leaders from across the country, all thirty states—no Faithers lived in the other twenty-three American states. Today, there are Faithers probably in only twenty of the fifty-three States.

All the old Orders merged into the New Protestant Order, and the Resistance became the Continuum. Today, the full Continuum is not only the New Protestant Order, but the new unified Jewish Orders, the Mormon Order, the African Collective, the Shogun, and the Magi.

Goth Lila is allowed into the large, open conference room by guards as the official first meeting of the year is ending. On the holo-walls are the faces of other attendees at locations within the United States and far outside the country. One of the faces is that of "General" Moses. The images degrade to billions of flashing green dots and then the vid-screens go dark.

Within moments, the Continuum members start vacating the meeting room. General Moses' wife—equally respected and followed by the Faither community—is also in the room. Her name is Emma, formally called "Mother Moses," but simply known by all as "M."

Strategic meetings are formal and planned months in advance. But the frequent tactical meetings are smaller and occur whenever and wherever they can pull everyone together. Their tactical street intel meeting begins immediately in the corner of the room; half are Goths. M joins them and gives Lila a shoulder hug from the side. All the preliminaries of the meeting have already been handled. Tactical teams never meet long; most times, they are held to physically exchange tek or quickly debrief. Palm tablets with the new protocols are passed out to everyone. The devices are disposals, and as soon as the information is reviewed and transferred, they will be physically destroyed.

"As of today, Goth Lila is point," Mikel says "We'll all be at our new African base."

"Enjoy your *vacation*, Mikel," says one of men.

Mikel laughs. "I'll be sure to send you the postcards."

As the group disperses, M turns to Lila. "I hope you know how much the Continuum and all its members appreciate you."

"I'm just doing my job like everyone else."

"Your group was far more disjointed at the start, before you took charge. We want you to know that your hard work is noticed. Noticed and appreciated. And I'd be remiss in my religious duties if I didn't also add that you are loved and blessed."

Goth Lila can't help but smile. "Thank you, M. I'm not good at compliments."

"I know. Your mission is as important as everyone else's. It's subtle, but will benefit the entire Continuum and all its people long after all of our separate missions are over. It's by no means a trivial thing. All your people must know that."

Goth Lila nods. "They know."

"Also, my husband is sorry he can't grant your request. He promised this Mr. Edison Blair that he would never use his in-country contacts to reach out to him again. You must find others."

"I understand. A promise is important."

"However, Moses has no doubt in your ability to track down anyone you set your sights on."

"When I do find him, does anyone want him for anything else?"

"No, but we are very interested. It was a loose thread from the '80s and we like to close the books on any loose threads. Did you talk to Goli already?"

"I did. He said to be very careful."

"Yes, the contractor who killed this boy's father is codenamed 'The Man Made Out of String.' Considering how the man died and that his home's security was fully active, I don't especially like that codename. Moses talked to this Edison Blair. He warned Logan to take his investigation seriously; he didn't and now he's dead."

"But this time we're the hunters."

"Maybe, but never underestimate your prey. That's why the Continuum is so good. Our enemies always underestimate us, but we never reciprocate. You have a mission to complete."

"Do you miss it yourself, going out on street missions?"

M smiles. "Every day."

Charleston, West Virginia
2:07 p.m., 9 January 2093

A fast-track speeds by on the elevated mono-rail at one hundred fifty miles an hour. It's a twenty-car bullet train painted in a camouflage design of greens, browns, and off-whites. The busy expressway is to its right with queues of ten cars each, one after another, bumper to bumper in auto-drive mode driving at nearly ninety-five miles an hour.

Like many New England states, West Virginia has a large population of expatriates from former Western Europe after it fell to the Islamic Caliphate in 2065. In the Virginias, there is an over-representation of expat British, so much so that this region is often called Neo-Britain or the NUK (Neo-United Kingdom). Other than English, a few other languages are heard among the passengers—talking on their mobile devices.

A young female passenger is slumped in her chair, her head resting against the window. She's dressed completely in white—top, jacket, dress, and boots. Even her short hair is white. Everyone in this section can see that she's in distress. The man sitting next to her cautiously stands, seeing the beads of sweat on her forehead, and sits in another seat.

It is rare, but sometimes a storm trooper policeman or two rides the line. Two of them enter the compartment from the back of the train. Their uniform is a light, motorcycle-type helmet with a clear eye shield and navy-colored, full body-armor. The body-armor is bulletproof, explosion-resistant, fully linked to the Net for enhanced power, and equipped with internal surveillance using all optics and audios, a complete interface with the Grid to coordinate tactical operations, internal climate control, a GPS link, and exo-skeleton strength enhancements.

One of the passengers sees them and points to the woman.

"Hello, Miss," says one of the policemen.

The woman doesn't respond until he repeats himself another two times. She seems weak, but manages to sit up. Her eyes are squinting so she covers them with dark glasses.

"Are you okay, Miss? Are you sick?"

"I'm not feeling well."

"How long have you been feeling this way?"

"It started when I got back home."

"From where?"

"I was out of the country…in the Asian Consortium. In Thailand, I think. I shouldn't have eaten that food. I should never have eaten that real meat. Don't eat anything but pure, synthetic meat." She seems to doze off.

"Miss, I'm going to swipe your skin with a swab." The policeman reaches over and a small applicator extends from his index finger. He swipes it across her hand and wrist. It retracts and he lifts up the palm display of his glove to his face.

Three seconds later, the policeman steps back and his visor goes from clear to black as the lower half of the faceplate wraps around the rest of his face. His partner activates the same on his helmet.

"Miss, please come with us. We have to call CDC." Passengers closest to them start to jump up from their seats. "Everyone just remain calm and stay in your seats. Miss, can you hear me?"

"What?" she asks. She looks up at them. "What's happening?"

"You're sick, but we've already called for help."

She starts to stand. "Okay…but my portfolio…I need to…"

"Don't worry about that, Miss. We'll get it for you." He turns to his partner. "We'll have to quarantine the whole train until we know who she has had contact with."

"No," the woman says. "I can't be kept here. I have to get…to my destination." She almost falls back, but is grabbed by the policeman.

"Just have a seat, Miss. We'll have medics waiting for you."

His partner taps him on the arm. The portfolio is open and they look at what's inside—reams of diagrams, maps, and formulas on sheets of digital paper marked "Top-Secret" in red. There are also pictures, but the one that catches their eyes shows some kind of light beam blowing up the moon.

"What are these documents, Miss?"

"No!" The woman jumps up, startling everyone. She grabs at the documents.

One policeman pushes her back as the other grabs her wrists. They handcuff her and set her back down on the seat. The policemen stand back as she fights to get out of the handcuffs. Every passenger, from the closest to those at the end of the car, is standing and watching.

The policemen pay her no attention. She can struggle until the next Ice Age; she'll never get out.

"Terminate!" she yells at the documents.

Smoke! The portfolio is crackling and the police open it again. The data on the digital paper sheets is erasing.

"Record," one of the policemen says to his helmet computer. The data is gone and the sheets catch on fire. The policemen throw the portfolio to the ground. One of them grabs a white-water cylinder from his holster and fires it to put out the flames.

The woman has passed out from all her struggling with the handcuffs.

The fast-track arrives on time at the station, but all the passengers are kept aboard as Centers for Disease Control personnel go car-to-car to verify that each person is free of any contaminants. Plenty of uniformed police are on the scene, along with drones in the air and media trying to get a story. The woman is strapped and shackled to a hover-gurney by government medics in bio-suits.

"She's not contagious, whatever it is," one medic says to another.

The medics gesture as a third one backs up the ambulance to them. The arresting policemen approach them.

"How much of those documents did you record?" asks one policeman.

"Hopefully enough for the teks to reconstruct it." The

policemen reach the medics. "Make sure she's not left alone," the policeman says to them. "In fact, we'll follow." He gestures to his partner.

"Officer, the woman is already dead," the medic says.

The policemen stop in place. "Is this a biological?" asks one of them.

"No, no. Not any kind of bio-terrorist attack. Whatever the contagion is, it is food-related, drug-related, or a mix."

"We need her identified—now," the other policeman says.

"We'll get you data as soon as we know. She's not in our registry, so she must be a foreign citizen."

The medics get the woman into the back of their ambulance. They secure the hover-gurney and close the door. *A minute passes, and the woman opens her eyes.*

Two medics get into the ambulance. As they drive out of the metro station, they look at the dashboard's rear compartment vid-screen and see the dead woman in the back. Ambulances are one of the only authorized vehicles, besides government police, that can bypass auto-drive.

The vehicle turns a corner and they hear something.

"What was that? Was that the door?"

They look at the vid-screen and it's dark. The driver slams on the brakes. The medics jump out and run to the back. The doors open. *It's empty.*

"Wasn't she dead?"

"We're in so much trouble."

The panicking medics backtrack on foot, looking all around as the Grid slows surrounding traffic to a stop.

Goth Lila has already taken off her white wig. She pulls off her facial mask. It takes her a minute to unpin her hair, shake it loose, and touch the buttons on her clothes—white turns to black.

The medics will look in vain. The police will review all surveillance from any Eyes or drone fly-bys in vain. She didn't jump out the back of the vehicle; it was her little android—and it flew out. She escaped the vehicle *before* the ambulance left. She leans back in the middle seats. There are two men, in the driver and passenger seats. The SUV continues to drive—they are already miles away.

Chapter Four: Bunny

New Harlem, New York
9:00 a.m., 3 February 2093

It is one of the upscale parts of New York. A few Presidents, over the decades, have had their offices here. Former President Kree Kanien was driven from office in 2072—twenty-one years ago. But the reason for his impeachment made him the most influential individual in NYC—the construction of the Three Towers.

To this day, he claims to be a staunch atheist, but he is the man, who, as President, directed federal troops to seize the site of One World Trade Center and its surrounding areas, and by executive order he commissioned its total demolition and the subsequent construction of the new one hundred and seventy-one story Three Towers. Not two towers, but three wider and taller towers—all because he heard "It." He said that days before, he heard a voice that told him to "build it so they will come and your army can destroy them."

Kanien claimed to be a descendant of a 9/11 victim, but no one in the media or government has ever been able to corroborate that claim. At the opening ceremony for the building, back in 2072, he invited and stood shoulder-to-shoulder with his fellow "Children of the Three Towers"—every direct descendant of every victim, thirty-thousand people present from America and nearly sixty other countries from around the world. After America, Old Britain, the Dominican Republic, and Japan had the next-highest losses in human lives. This was Kanien's "army," and even back then he said he had a million members. Today his organization, or cult, has tens of millions—a cult in wait for the end of the world. An End triggered by an attack on the Three Towers.

It is for this reason that he has been formally designated by Homeland as a terrorist. Not for current or past activities or plots, but for *future* ones. They are afraid of what he freely admits he will do if the Towers are ever attacked—seize control of New York, appoint himself its sole Emperor, and destroy the attackers. But he's an ex-President, with a current government security detail at taxpayers' expense. The joke is that at least half of the New York Police Department are associate members of his Children of the Three Towers. President T. Wilson is the President of the United States, but not in New York.

Kanien is an old man, but half of all Americans will live past a hundred. He moves around via hover-wheelchair; he can walk, but his legs are weak and he doesn't want cybernetic ones or new organic ones grown in a body-farm. Despite his physical frailties, he has a magnetic personality and still has a booming voice.

His Harlem offices take up the entire penthouse floor of the three-story building. The second floor has the secure offices of his Secret Service detail, and the bottom floor houses his Presidential Library. Every employee of his cult organization wears the symbol "III" on his or her person. Those in business dress wear it on necklaces or rings, while the casually dressed ones wear T-shirts with the symbol.

The elevator opens on the main penthouse offices and the six-foot-tall Bunny, with her six-inch heels, walks out. Today, she's dressed in blue with her coat draped over one arm and her dark glasses in her left hand. She waves hello as she passes the receptionist station staffed by two female receptionists and one male security agent to the side. The biometric sensor automatically opens the main entrance door for her.

As she walks to her office, she sees that Kanien is in a meeting with several people in office suits. Kanien spends most of his days in meetings; he's the consummate planner, organizer and fundraiser. All the offices have glass walls, and she can see who's in and what everyone is doing at a glance.

She used to be a very chatty person in life, but here it's all work. Kanien hires based on looks, but you keep your job based on work. She's the only senior executive "non-Child" of the Three Towers organization. Three hours in and she's answered most of the high-level messages to President Kanien and flagged and sent the important few to his to-do file for him to personally respond to—people Kanien will be able to work his "magic" on for larger donations.

"Ms. Bunny." She turns to see one of the Secret Service agents at her door.

"Yes."

"A word."

She puts her desk computer on "nap" as he enters and closes the glass door. He sits down. None of Kanien's detail smiles and not one of them has ever made a pass at her, which has always made her wonder about their sexuality—or if they are androids, but she appreciates their unflappable professionalism. Kanien has the best of the best working for him.

"What is it, agent?"

The man unfolds his collapsible palm tablet. "An individual by the name of…Sprocket has set up an appointment with you through the front desk, even though we told him that there was no such person working here. He knows that you do and will be here this afternoon."

"I don't know anyone by that name."

"Ms. Bunny, we know you are very diligent in keeping your personal life away from work. We have never had even one incident from you in the years you've been with the President."

"Thank you."

"You're welcome. This Sprocket said that you would take the meeting once I told you who he was."

"I doubt that."

"He says he's Logan's son."

Bunny freezes in place. She looks away, and has to catch herself from starting to cry.

"I take it that you will be having the meeting," the agent says.

Bunny closes her eyes for a moment and clears her throat. "Yes…but…well, I don't have to tell you how to do your job. You know it better than I do."

"He'll be searched and scanned thoroughly."

Bunny makes eye contact again. "Did you already look him up in the Registry?"

The Registry was the national identity file for every citizen and resident of America, alive or dead, including every data point—financial history, medical history, criminal history, etc.

"We did." Bunny doesn't have to ask the next question. "He has the same designation as his biological parent, who is deceased—domestic terrorist." The agent smiles. "Half the people in this building, including President Kanien, have that same designation. Such labels don't carry much weight with us until we do our own independent investigation and assessment. We'll keep it all confidential."

"Thank you, agent."

Albert Einstein Center, Virginia
11:00 a.m., 3 February 2093

All along the office wall are various models of humanoid robots. A picture of an android Albert Einstein hangs on the adjacent wall. The office's owner doesn't even look like a scientist, wearing a T-shirt and skin jeans, and his long, graying black hair rests on his shoulders. He looks through clear glasses at the two men in black suits.

"What number am I?" asks the scientist.

"Excuse me?" the agent asks.

"You all have your own in-house scientists, so I'm obviously not the first scientist you've met with."

"We've talked to a lot, sir."

"Then why do you think I will say anything different from them?"

"We want to be thorough."

"I looked at the file you sent and I don't know what you think it proves. Where do you government types come up with such conspiratorial plots? You really think someone is building some space death weapon that can destroy the moon?"

"Or maybe just a major tek-city."

"Did it ever occur to you that these anarchists, terrorists, or whatever, are taking you along for a ride?"

"Yes, we have, but we have many facts that, when all taken together, lead us to believe that there is something here."

"I don't know what to tell you. My review is no different from that of your in-house people. I believe it's all impossible to create, and my personal opinion is that it's all a hoax."

"You seem very emphatic about it, sir. This is a national security issue—"

The scientist laughs. "Do you think if I thought someone, anyone, could build some wormhole, space death-ray, laser-beam, planet-killer weapon that I wouldn't say so? The planet dies and I do too, if that happens. It's not real. None of it is. Someone is intentionally leading you on a goose chase, or they're crazy, or maybe you stole someone's movie script."

One agent laughs. "We can assure you it's not the latter."

"If you say so. Well, tell the President for me that he has nothing to worry about."

New Harlem Offices of President Kanien
2:00 p.m., 3 February 2093

"Please leave my goggles on," Sprocket says. "They're not death rays."

One agent physically pats down his body while another scans him with a hand-scanner device. A third agent watches him.

"Please sir, remove the goggles and hand them to us."

"Johnnie-o, you're really annoying me." Sprocket closes his eyes as he takes them off and hands them to one of the agents. The tint is very slight. The agents inspect and scan them before putting them back in his hand.

Sprocket snuggly secures them back over his eyes. "Anything else?"

The third agent says, "Sir, please accompany my agents to the latrine so that we can do the full-body cavity search."

Sprocket bursts out laughing. "No finger dancing with my privates, Johnnie-o! I don't need to meet with her that badly."

The third agent gives him a robotic smile. "A little Secret Service humor," he says without the slightest sign of emotion.

"You're good," Sprocket says. "With that kind of emotional control, you could make a lot of digi-cash on the comedy circuit. You had me ready to start a marathon-long foot chase away from you guys."

Sprocket is led into a small glass-walled conference room where Bunny is already seated and waiting.

"You're BB Bunny," Sprocket says.

Bunny laughs. "I haven't been called that in a long time."

"What does the BB stand for?"

"Bouncin' Bodacious."

"That's you all right." Sprocket takes a seat as the agents close the door and stand outside. "You're like eight feet tall."

"I have to say I don't see the resemblance."

"You mean me and my bio-dad?"

"I don't see it. And you don't seem too serious about the whole thing."

Sprocket's playful demeanor disappears. "What happened to him?"

"He got killed. What do you think?"

"By who?"

"What does it matter? You can't do anything about it."

"Tell me anyway."

Her eyes begin to tear up. "I think this meeting is over. I can't imagine Logan would have a son like you."

She's passed judgment on me in three seconds. "The only thing I need from you is Edison Blair's location."

"How do you know him?"

"I know my bio-dad worked for him and not you, the office help. He did tell me about Edison, you, and your headquarters in Arlington, Virginia."

Bunny has to close her eyes as the emotions well up inside

again.

"I'm sorry," Sprocket says. "I'm a playful guy, but you wanted me to be jerky. Just tell me how to contact Edison and I'm gone. You'll never see me again."

"It won't matter if you are able to find him, but I don't know where he is."

"I can't believe that you have no way to contact him."

"Well, I don't."

"Give me something. I'm not going to drop this. Let my bio-dad end his existence as just a name on the deceased persons' registry. That's not right. Get me to Edison and Edison and I will figure something out."

Bunny smiles. "You and Edison. We were more Logan's family than you were."

"That's why I'm going to do something while you two hide like hairy Trog-land garbage rodents."

"Shut-up. The only thing that will happen to you is that you'll end up dead too."

"Good! I'll be in good company. My bio-dad and me. Not you two hairy Trog rodents."

"Shut up!"

"You shut up!"

The glass door opens and one of the agents peeks in. "Everything alright, Ms. Bunny?"

She takes her glare off Logan's son and looks up. "Everything is okay."

The agent pops back out.

"I'll give you what you want. So you'll get exactly what you want and deserve," she says.

"Anything will help. The President killed my bio-dad; is that what you're suggesting by not telling me?"

"The current one, not my boss. You do have some brains. Maybe you did get some of Logan's genes. Hopefully not the wrong ones."

"Wrong ones?"

"The ones that tell you when to run and you don't do it."

"I don't have that problem. Where's Edison? Is he here in America or somewhere else?"

"He's in Caliphate territory."

"Muslims? Why would he hide there? Isn't he Old British? They super-hate Muslims. Why couldn't he be in the Russian Bloc, CHIN territory, or Spanish Americas?"

"Are you afraid someone will make you one of their virgin brides?" Bunny laughs to herself.

"They make my neck itch. I am *not* happy now."

"Changed your mind?"

"No chance. I'm not stopping until I'm as close to Edison as I am to you."

"You have no chance of getting there. No chance."

"How did I find you? My friends are Jew-Christians and they will get me wherever I need to go."

"Jew-Christians? They were the ones who got him into Caliphate territory."

Sprocket is surprised. "Then they'll get me there too. What do I need to do? Edison and I have some revenge to plot together."

Kanien's Executive Office
6:22 p.m., 3 February 2093

The third agent stands in front of him. President Kanien sits in his hover-chair behind his huge desk.

"Is Ms. Bunny going to help him?"

"She is, sir. The man is the biological child of a man named

Logan, whom she worked with before for many years. Not sure if there was any sexual relationship, but definitely an emotional attachment. This Logan was on the administration termination list in '89."

Kanien is intrigued.

"The son is on the terrorism watch list," the agent continues.

"As am I, and every other American the administration doesn't like," Kanien says.

"Yes, sir."

"Are there any current warrants on him now?"

"Currently, none. Looks like he's kept off the Grid for the last three years, but Grid surveillance will, of course, alert them that he's now or was in NYC."

"Do you think what he's doing could cause any 'discomfort' to our current President? He is so focused on this upcoming world superpower summit with the Russians."

"I think President T. Wilson would be very displeased with what he's planning."

"Then make sure all NYC vid-files are erased so that he was never here. We still control the feed here don't we?"

"Yes we do, sir."

"Good." Kanien smiles. "This young man can't be acting alone."

"We think he's being helped by Jew-Christians."

"Ha!" Kanien almost stands up from his hover-chair. "I'm a terrorist. He's a terrorist. He's being helped by a terrorist people. This is all too good. Erase the vid-files and maybe plant a false trail somewhere else. What's the Vice President's state again?"

"California."

"Plant the trail there."

"Yes, sir."

"I so like being an agent of chaos to my former understudy Mr. Torrey Wilson. Soon they'll be calling me a Jew-Christian. Best we start building bridges to those people. When the world's end comes, the Children of the Three Towers will become the Army of the Three Towers, and we will need many allies to create the new world order."

Chapter Five: Haggard

Unknown Location, Mexico
8:22 p.m., 7 February 2093

Sprocket stands on the covered dock, wearing a plastic bubble-jacket, a wool-knit cap, and rubber combat boots. He has "graduated" to a new yellow tint for his goggles. He looks up. The entire dock is inside a mountain cave; the walls and ceiling are perfectly smooth. He wonders how long it took machines to carve out the massive man-made cave.

The dock has only one ship; no name is visible on its bluish outer hull. It is a large ship at three stories, not including the deck, with small port windows lining each level. People are everywhere: some directing cargo container bots into the open center hold of the ship, some armed and stationed to watch the perimeter, and others arriving in vehicles to join the crew.

There are a lot of cargo containers. He wonders what they could be, but he knows better than to ask. He looks up and stares at the ceiling. Something caught his eye. After a few moments, he can see its shape—the Jew-Christians have camouflaged drones. He wonders how many are hovering.

Goth Lila appears, walking out of the ship's center hold to him.

Sprocket has been standing by himself with his belongings for the trip—one big duffel bag and a smaller satchel. They had confiscated all his tek devices.

Goth Lila stops in front of him. "There is no shame in turning back to go home," she says.

He smiles and shakes his head. "Not a chance. Three years and I almost killed myself. I'm not stopping now."

"You do understand how dangerous this trip will be?"

"I'm not scared. I'm with you. The Anarchists and Nihilists wouldn't be scared of all of you for nothing. I know why the Vampires are scared of you. I'll be okay." Lila watches him. "Oh, one of your people said that if I called someone a Jew-Christian that I might get punched in the face. What do I call you? Isn't Jew-Christian the name of your religion?"

"Jews and Christians are separate religions."

"But you all always work together."

"Yes, but we are separate religions. Similar, but separate, and our faith is very important to us. And…we pray to the same God. Does that make sense to you?"

"Yes."

"Use the word Faithers. I don't have time to give you a theology lesson on Jews, Christians, Catholics, and all the rest we call Faithers."

"Is the word 'Faither' religious?"

"It's a political term. Think of it as a synonym for the Resistance."

"I understand now."

"Once you go aboard and we sail, that's it."

"I'm ready. I've been ready."

"Let me see what you're wearing."

She looks him over.

"You need a code name," she says.

"What's your code name?" he asks.

"I'll tell you when I know you better." She thinks for a moment. "You look like a rube."

"And that is?"

She smiles. "Not too sophisticated. Not from the tek-city."

Sprocket laughs. "That's fine with me if it's something you can easily remember."

"How are you sleeping?"

"I'm sleeping good now."

She sees no reason to correct his grammar. "Have you ever been on a boat or ship?"

"No, this will be my first time."

Lila shakes her head. "I hope you're not a wobbly-willie and go throwing up all over the place."

"Why would I do that?"

"Seasickness?"

"They got drugs for that."

Lila stops and glares at him.

"I'm just joking, joking. I'm not a seasickness person. I've done a lot of dirt surfing before."

"That is not the same thing. But it's too late now. We're going."

He grabs his bags and follows her to the ship.

"How long will it take to get there?"

"Mr. Sprocket, we have to go to the other side of the world, avoiding government surveillance, pirates—"

"Pirates? There are real pirates on the ocean? This is going to be a great trip!"

"I'll remember you said that when they start shooting at us."

"We'll be gone awhile then."

"Yes."

"So what religion are you? And what religions are here?"

"Interested in religion now, Mr. Sprocket?"

"I just want to know, as long as there are no Muslims."

She looks at him. "You do remember where we're going."

"That's different."

"The crew is Christian. My people and I are Christian. The rest are Jews, some Catholics, and even another Pagan."

Sprocket smiles. "Another Godless guy. Great! I got a hangout buddy."

Lila laughs. "Hangout? Mr. Haggard doesn't *hang out*, and he's no one's buddy."

The Ship
8:31 p.m., 7 February 2093

The crewman shows Sprocket to his quarters. It's a small room with bedroom, bathroom, study, and kitchenette all in one. Before he can say thanks, the crewman is gone, closing the door behind him.

He sits on his bunk and looks around. No vid-screen entertainment here. *This is going to be a long trip.*

It's bedtime. Sprocket lies in the bunk, staring at the ceiling. He hasn't felt any movement in the ship, but it's been hours and they must have already departed. It's too quiet. He had the light off to sleep, but had to turn it back on—he felt like he was in a coffin. He sits up. There is no way he can sleep in this room.

He gets up and puts on his slippers. When he opens the door, the lights are brighter and his goggles adjust. Even before he can walk down the hallway, he sees an armed crewman at the far end of the hall. The man walks to him.

Lila arrives and walks to a waiting Sprocket, now with two crewman guards standing with him. She is not happy.

"What is it?"

"I just wanted to take a walk."

"Sprocket, this is not a vacation cruise, this is a military operation."

"Can't I take a walk?"

"What are you wearing on your feet? If the emergency alarms sounded and you had to get to the main deck, how effective would your escape for your life be with your velvet playboy slippers? Your boots at all times. Why aren't you sleeping, anyway?"

"I can't sleep in there."

"Why?"

"It's too quiet. Can't you put me in the crew sleeping quarters? I saw them on the way to my room."

"It's a cabin, not a room. We thought you'd like your own space."

"No, I can't sleep like this. Put me with the crew."

"Are you sure?"

"Yeah."

"You may hear men praying or see them reading Bibles and other atrocities."

Sprocket laughs to himself. *She's always trying to provoke me.* "I'll survive."

Sprocket gets comfortable in his double bunk bed. The bed above is empty. The sleeping quarters are much larger than his previous cabin, with three rows of double bunks. The men are talking—though he doesn't know what language it is, getting their uniforms ready for the next shift, polishing their boots by hand—machines can do that, he thinks—and playing solitaire. Some men are sleeping and he sees a few reading physical books with crosses on them. He's never seen a Bible, so he assumes that's what the books are.

He removes his goggles and, while keeping his eyes closed, collapses them and puts them under his pillow. He can feel the sleep coming as he covers his head with his light blanket.

Third Day

He has his routine set now. The crews work eight hours on, then sixteen hours off, overlapping shifts. He has no official duties at all, except for his own personal routine of walking down the full length of the ship in the morning when he wakes up. The middle deck contains the living quarters, but he doesn't know what's on the top and below decks. The command deck is obviously above and cargo is kept below, but that leaves a lot of other space. He is always friendly to his cabin mates with a "hi" or "good day." They respond, but it's clear that English isn't their first language or that they even speak English.

The cafeteria always has the best food. Everything is fresh, and he's eaten a wider variety of seafood these past three days than he's had his entire life. Usually when he arrives, the cafeteria is empty; he's just missed the previous shift and it will be hours before the next.

His "care pack" arrived on the second day. An old tablet loaded with thousands of books—no Net connection of course—and an equal number of vid-games. That's what he does all day, read and play vid-games. The digital books are in almost every genre. He likes the mysteries and spy novels. He's surprised by how violent some of the vid-games are for Faithers, but that's what he prefers.

Seventh Day

Sprocket finally learned the crew's schedule so that he wouldn't be eating alone during meals. He also found the rec-rooms—sitting areas for conversation and drinks, card tables (where games of poker and blackjack were the norm), chess, pool tables, and multi-player vid-games. People did their reading in their cabins; the rec-room was for socializing. In Tek World, direct human socializing isn't a necessity and not even considered the desired form of contact—that's what tek is for. Here, personal social interaction is a daily practice.

He finds out what Goth Lila meant. He meets Mr. Haggard. In his late seventies, the man is physically imposing. Sprocket learns that he used to be a boxer and distinguished himself in the boxing world by beating opponents to unconsciousness, never losing a match.

They sit at the card table, the seven of them. Sprocket, Haggard, and one other man are the only ones still in the game.

"What language do you speak besides English?" Sprocket asks.

"Why?" the dark-skinned man asks.

"Maybe I can learn a bit while I'm on this trip."

"I doubt you'll want to do that. I speak Hebrew, Russian, Chinese, Hindi, Arabic, and Farsi."

"I'll raise you two hundred," Sprocket says.

The man watches Sprocket put the chips into the center of the table and then glance up with a smile.

Sprocket adds, "We can see your 'tell' when you're distracted."

Haggard chuckles as he throws two hundred worth of chips into the "pot."

The man smiles too as he shakes his head slowly. "So which language should I curse at you in?" He throws down his cards.

"Doesn't matter to me. I can't understand any of them."

"Okay, Mr. Sprocket, let's get this over with," Haggard says. Just the two of them left in the game.

"I'm quite good, you know. You old-timers always underestimate youth."

Haggard wins all of Sprocket's chips in the next round.

Sixteenth Day

It may be a military mission, but Sprocket enjoys his casual, vacation-like existence. Haggard doesn't have any formal duties either, but he's some kind of Very Important Person, whether it has to do with the cargo, the ship, or the purpose of the mission, Sprocket doesn't know. Then there are the Jews, who are always below, except when they come up for meals. They interact with the crew, but avoid him. There's Rachel Glick, about his age, petite, with very fair skin and shoulder-length brown hair. The rest of her "team" are the same age or younger, both male and female. They know he watches them.

"What's down below?" he asks when he's back in his bunk reading from his tablet.

One of his cabin mates in the double bunk next to him asks, "Why?"

"Is it a secret?"

"It is," the man answers with his accent. "You are a passenger, not part of the crew. You don't need to know anything about the ship or crew for us to take you to your destination."

No answers from him.

Twenty-First Day

The alarms jolt him from his bunk. He only fell asleep moments ago, and he thinks he was having a normal dream. It takes him seconds to put on his goggles. Lila told him he didn't need them while aboard and inside, but he likes them. If he's going to be a secret agent with a code name, he needs an accessory.

It is the first time he can feel that he's on a ship at sea by the slight roll. All the men in the sleeping quarters are dressed and run out to their stations. Sprocket gets his boots and jacket on; he sleeps with most of his clothes on, as told, like the rest of his shipmates.

He runs into the hallway, but unlike every other time there are no guards. The hall lights are flashing red and he thinks he hears a loud noise above. He knows where it is. Down the hall to the door to the stairwell, through the door, and up the steps he goes. One level, the next, and then he stops at the final door to the main deck. He was on board a full two weeks when he first learned that the ship wasn't just a ship but a submersible. They haven't been sailing the seas, they've been sailing underwater. The indicator shows green; red would mean that they were submerged.

"Green light," he says to himself and pushes the door open.

The rush of fresh air is both freezing and exhilarating. He hasn't been outside in all this time. His face is hit by the sting of water. At first he thinks it is water washing across the deck, but now he realizes that they are in a raging storm. The sky is dark. He hears an explosion and sees a flash of light to his left.

He leaves the cover of the exit door and moves farther onto the deck. Without the ship's hand-holds, he would have fallen on his backside and been tossed across the deck—maybe even overboard. He is so glad he has his goggles, as the rain is fierce. He makes his way, hand-hold to hand-hold, toward the center of the ship to see what the explosions are.

As he nears the main railing to look overboard, he sees them. Several smaller ships are a few hundred feet away; three of them are totally engulfed in flames. One near the center explodes and sinks into the ocean. He is caught off guard and shakes as seemingly every gun turret on the ship fires at the remaining ships. They return fire.

Something is buzzing around up in the air. *Is it drones?* Photo-flares explode and the buzzing is revealed to be dozens of people flying through the air with rocket-packs. There is no uniform or dress common to all of them other than they are all armed, and wearing body-armor and combat helmets. One of them sees him and dives.

"Oh—" Sprocket knows he can't get away. He drops to the cold, hard deck.

The intruder lands and starts to aim his tek-rifle at him. *Bam!* The sound startles Sprocket. The intruder's head jerks back from a bullet through the center of his helmet. The intruder falls back and disappears, swept across the deck by the rolling of the ship in these rough waters.

Sprocket turns his head. Haggard stands there holding his old-style handgun. It looks like a .44 Magnum, but Sprocket can't be sure. Old tek demolishes new tek. Haggard is angry; he grabs Sprocket and lifts him up as though he weighs nothing. Sprocket is thrown and flies through the door to land on the ground inside the ship. Haggard steps back in and slams the door.

"How did you get on the deck?!"

"I walked out the door."

Sprocket now finds himself surrounded by armed crewmen.

"I didn't know I couldn't go on the deck. I only wanted to see what was happening."

Haggard stands over him and seems to be debating with himself. He pulls Sprocket up.

When the elevator opens, Sprocket finds himself on what must be the main bridge. There are a couple dozen men of different nationalities at stations, most look to be native African. There is a complete view of the battle taking place around the ship. Sprocket doesn't ask and runs to one side of the observation windows.

The ship's gun-turrets are firing in all directions at the swarm of flying rocket-pack-wearing invaders. All he sees are tiny explosions in the air as one intruder after another is hit. He hears a different sound from the other side of the bridge and runs there to barely catch sight of the missile being launched. It lands in the middle of two ships and the explosion is so large that the vessels are lifted into the air as they explode.

The bridge crew is amused as they watch Sprocket enjoy the "show," but keep their focus on their station displays.

The elevator opens and Rachel and her team exit. She immediately notices Sprocket and is surprised. She looks at Haggard, who gives her a smirk.

Sprocket's head is rubber-necking in every direction as he tries to follow every shot and explosion. The sky lights up and lightning strikes an aircraft that, up until that moment, was invisible to him. The aircraft shorts out, catches fire, and crashes into the ocean.

"Did you see that?" Sprocket yells. "The lightning took out that plane!"

The battle is over and Sprocket now takes notice of the crew. Haggard is amused, the crew is apathetic, and Rachel and her team are annoyed. Then he sees Goth Lila. Sprocket straightens up.

"You're fighting pirates now," she says.

"Those were pirates?" He tries to remove the smile from his face.

"How did you get on the deck?"

"I walked out the door."

"You would have had to go up two levels to walk out the door.

What if we were submerged?"

"The door wouldn't have opened and there would have been a red light."

Lila looks at the Captain. "Weren't all the doors locked down?"

"Miss, he got out before internal access was disabled. He probably opened it one second before."

Lila looks at Sprocket again, annoyed.

"No one told me," Sprocket says.

"You hear explosions and you run *to* them?"

"Well…yeah."

She points to the three men behind her. "These are your new *buddies*. They will make sure you don't get yourself into any more trouble."

"This was just one time. I'm not causing trouble. Just tell me what to do."

"Don't leave your level. Don't go on the deck unless you ask me first. Run away from, not to, explosions. Don't fight armed pirates."

"I didn't know we were fighting pirates." He covers his mouth to hide his laughter.

"I always seem to get the comedians whenever I take civilians on missions." She looks at the men behind her. "Take Mr. Sprocket back to his quarters."

He grudgingly follows them.

"Are we close?' he stops to ask her.

"We're close, and that means more danger."

Sprocket follows the men into the elevator and it closes.

"What is that person doing on this ship?" Rachel asks.

"He's been cleared," Lila says.

"Cleared? He's not part of the mission. He shouldn't even be here. Do you know the kind of cargo we have onboard? Why couldn't you have taken a dedicated vessel for your mission?"

"There wasn't time."

"The League has significant cargo aboard not only for the Jewish Orders, but the Christian Orders as well."

"I know that. It won't be much longer. He'll depart and he'll be gone. This ship doesn't have just one mission. We all have our own missions to accomplish."

"We're in the Indian Ocean now, and there will be more pirate attacks and who knows what issues we'll have to deal with in terms of the regional governments. The League's mission takes precedence."

The League of Artifacts, Curios, Curiosities, Mementos, Relics, and Antiquities; the secret society of Faithers formed within Washington DC's Smithsonian, and founded by a Pagan—Mr. John Haggard. The League had one specific mission: to protect all artifacts, documents, and antiquities of a religious nature.

Mr. Haggard looks at the Captain. "Any damage to my boat?"

"Minimal, sir."

"Get the maintenance bots on it. I always keep my things in perfect order." As the Captain has his crew task the robots, he turns to Lila. "What's so important about this kid? Why did the Continuum approve your mission with him?"

"We have a specific purpose for him. We have an open case file and we want to bring it to resolution."

"And he has to go all the way to Islamic Caliphate territory to do it?"

"Yes."

Haggard continues, "Let me be blunt, Lila. I don't want anything to jeopardize the League's mission. It does take precedence. I think your mission is ill-advised and that the Continuum is spreading itself too thin. Do you even have enough resources to get him in there and back out safely?"

"We do."

"Those resources wouldn't be the IRA, would they?"

Lila doesn't answer.

"If you're comfortable putting your fate in the hands of Muslims, then you are braver than I," Haggard says.

"Who else would we use in Caliphate territory? This is a critical mission."

"It must be," Haggard says. "I might as well tell you now, but there's supposed to be some kind of world summit being planned to be hosted by the Russian Bloc. The leaders of America, the Caliphate, and the CHINs are in talks to attend. What that means for you and me is that the CHINs and the Caliphate, since we're nearing their territory, are cracking down on all internal dissidents. Your mission plans may not be as set as you think."

"We have to proceed. This mission is directly related to Project Noah."

Haggard and Rachel express surprise.

"I can't say more," Lila says.

"I see," Haggard says. "But be ready to alter your mission plans at a moment's notice. Pirates are nothing. We have to watch out for countries, and this region is about to get very *interesting* for us before we're done."

Thirtieth Day

Last week was some Jew-Christian holiday called Christmas. In fact, the whole month of March seems to have one religious holiday after another for the Faithers. Sprocket lies on his bunk with his eyes closed and his forearm resting on his forehead. Someone shakes him awake.

Sprocket wakes up right away and instinctively grabs his goggles to put on. He fastens them and sits up.

"Get dressed and bring all your bags," Goth Lila says. "We disembark in ten minutes. The mission is scrapped. We're sending you home."

Chapter Six: Edison Blair

The Ship
10:57 p.m., 8 March 2093

Sprocket is furious as he paces back and forth. They are in the main bridge's adjacent briefing room. Goth Lila stands with a few of her people, the Captain with some of his officers, and Mr. Haggard.

"I am not going back after we've come all this way," he says. "We're here. We're already here."

"You are not listening," Lila says. "The CHINs shot down a Caliphate jet they said strayed into their airspace and there is a blockade in place by both empires. We can't get to our rendezvous point."

"I don't care. I can jump overboard and swim there."

"Sir, they would pluck you right out of the water," the Captain says.

Haggard looks at Lila. "You need to make a decision because we can't stay here any longer. We have to go."

"What about going through the Russian Bloc?"

"It'll take too long. We'll miss the rendezvous. If that happens, Edison Blair will be gone. It could be years or more before we reacquire him."

"Why can't I fly in? From an airport. I can just fly into one of the local airports, take the metro lines, and get there. I'll be a tourist."

"You're an American, sir," the Captain says. "How will you explain your sudden appearance at their airport without the proper passport codes?"

"I was on a boat and we came ashore and decided to see the pyramids. That's a tourist destination."

"It's too dangerous," Lila says.

"I'm willing to risk it."

"Mr. Sprocket, it will not be just your life at stake."

"Tell me where to go and I'll do it on my own. You don't have to take me."

"Somehow I doubt you will do well on your own in a Muslim country."

"I'll do it. Tell me where to go and everything, and I'll make it. I can do it. I can."

Lila looks at the crew.

"We have to go, Lila," Haggard says again.

"He'll need money," Lila says. Haggard takes a digi-card from his wallet and hands it to her. "He can't carry a gun, but it's common for people to carry knives."

One of the crew members takes a knife from his waist holster and hands it to Sprocket. "I want it back. It's an Arabic family heirloom and is older than your own country."

"Can we risk a surrogate?" she asks, referring to a robot that is linked to a human operator and unable to function independently.

The Captain shakes his head. "Outside the main tek-cities, people don't like robots at all. It'll draw too much attention to him, but we can do a live link with his goggles. It'll be as if you're right next to him."

"Like a guardian angel." She looks up to see a smiling Sprocket looking back at her. He reaches out his hand for the digi-card. She hands it to him.

"I can do it," he says again.

Madagascar
6:15 a.m., 9 March 2093

The African country is just outside the blockade area. The ocean is dotted with Caliphate warships. He takes his small shuttle boat into the port by himself. He is wearing very loose clothing, his goggles, and a new baseball cap; he blends into the crowds. The only bag he can take is a knapsack, which he wears in front of his body, rather than behind. Gypsies and pickpockets can empty it in seconds, and wearing it in front shows that you're not a "stupid tourist," but rather a street-smart one. People are almost right on top of each other. The smells (good food, strong perfumes, and not-so-nice body odor), and an array of languages he's never heard before.

It wasn't until he got into his shuttle boat that he saw the name of Haggard's boat—*The Prestige*. Wherever it is, it's long gone and he probably will never see it or its crew again. He buys passage on a boat and has to wait until it fills up with other passengers. There are lots of men wearing turbans, fezzes, and *keffiyehs* (what Americans would say is "that towel on their head"). Lots of women with burkahs (can't see their face) and hijabs (can see their face). People glance at him from time to time. With his lighter skin, they assume he's Russian or East Europan.

The boat doesn't depart for another three hours. Despite its small size, it's a speed-craft and quickly makes its way up to the Arabian Sea. He embarks at their first stop in Yemen; the boat will continue up the Red Sea with its final stop in Egypt.

Sprocket waits on the street near one of the many eateries. It's as busy as every other street—lots of people traffic, people playing table games he's unaware of, dogs everywhere—and then he sees a new animal being walked down the street by a man in a turban.

"What's that?" he asks. "Is that a genetically engineered animal?"

"You've never seen a camel before?" Lila's voice sounds in his ear-set.

"But look at it. I bet those big humps are for extra water storage."

"Camels have been around for millions of years; that's before people. Hey—stay back. Don't pet them, they bite hard."

Sprocket moves back and smiles as the man passes with the animal. "I would have bet that they were genetically engineered. They're perfect for this area."

"Yes, God can be smart like that."

11:05 a.m.

It's like when he was on stakeout tracking Lila. Though, this time there will be no "zombies." He continues to sit, waiting and watching. The heat is unbearable, but the people around him are going about their lives as if it's nothing.

A man comes out of the crowd and walks up to him.

"Who are you?" he asks.

"Who are you?" Sprocket asks back.

"This is my country, foreigner."

"I am hot and I'm about to pass out. Don't you guys know that there is such a thing as air-regulators in the world? Just take me where you need to take me and get me into some shade."

"My people need no such machines. We are people of the sun, not weak like you. How do I know you are him?"

"The magic word is Edison Blair. Let's go. I'm dying in this heat."

Sprocket stands as the man looks him over, then reluctantly leads him away.

The covered jeep has been driving for as long as he was sitting there waiting. Sprocket is sprawled out in the back. The man is in the passenger's seat and another burly man drives.

"Who else is listening to us?" the man asks without turning around in his seat.

"Goth Lila," her voice booms from the speaker in Sprocket's goggles.

"Hello Miss…it is Mrs. now, isn't it?"

"It is."

"Mrs. Goth Lila, it is too bad we weren't able to meet. We hear so much about certain people in the Resistance, but we get to meet so few."

"One day we might."

"If God is willing, yes," he says. "What is the story with this pale-face with me? Why am I driving him to where I'm driving him?"

"He is known by your friend."

"I hope he is because if my friend doesn't know him, we'll kill him and leave him in the desert for the vultures."

Sprocket sits up straight.

"I'd expect no less," Lila's voice says.

"Is this the only thing you need from my friend?"

"Just one other thing, but it will require both your passenger and your friend to complete."

"What do we get in return?"

"What do you need?"

"The IRA needs many things."

"Then we'll talk off-line."

"We're almost to our base. Pale-face won't be able to take any tek in there."

"Then I'll talk to you when I talk to you."

He says something in another language. "Good-bye Mrs. Goth Lila and May God be with you."

"God be with you, too."

The line disconnects and the man reaches back with his open hand. Sprocket takes the attachment off his goggles and puts it in the man's hand.

2:35 p.m.

Sprocket has never seen or been in a desert and plans never to set foot in one again. His skin is baking in the heat and his body is covered in sand. He sits on the ground with about a dozen men standing and circling him. The area is covered in large dome tents. His contact went into one, but that was about an hour ago.

Why does everything take so long in this part of the world?

His contact comes out, and right behind him is a humanoid robot. It squats down and looks into Sprocket's face. It must be a surrogate—*controlled by Edison Blair?*

"I'm Logan's son, and I'm here to see Edison Blair."

The robot stands and nods to the man as it walks back into the dome tent.

"Stand, Pale-Face," his contact commands.

Since his contact has a nickname for him, he'll do the same. His contact will be Mr. Wild Hair. It was something his bio-dad always did. Give people names, much easier to remember them.

Wild Hair scans him one last time with a device, then leads him into the dome tent. Inside it is dimly lit. He can barely see, but there are quite a number of people there, all sitting on a large rug that takes up the entire dimensions of the tent. His contact points Sprocket to a spot in front of a silhouetted person. Sprocket sits as he takes off his baseball cap.

The person in front of him is doing the same thing as almost everyone else next to him—smoking from a hookah pipe. With each inhale, the pipe glows a subtle yellow, but dim enough not to reveal the full image of his face.

"Sprocket," the man in front of him says.

"Yes."

"You're a long way from America."

"I am, a very long way. I thought the trip would never end." Sprocket notices his contact is still standing behind him. He looks back to the man.

"Do you want any refreshments?" the silhouetted man in front of him asks.

"Yes, can I have some water? That would be great."

One of the shadowy people in front of Sprocket hands him something. Sprocket can't really see what it is, but hears the water sloshing around inside. It's some kind of animal hide water bottle. He figures out that the tip is the opening and hangs it upside down to drink. The water is so cold and good. In a few moments, it's all gone.

Wild Hair takes the water bottle.

"That was good. Thank you."

"Why are you here, Mr. Sprocket? Why did they send you?"

"No one sent me. I sent myself. Are you Edison Blair?"

"Why don't you pretend I am, for the sake of this conversation?"

"I've been tracking you. I found the Jew-Christian—I mean the Faither—who I knew could help me. Then I found Bunny. Now I'm here. I want to know exactly how my bio-dad was killed. I want to know everything. What, where, how, and who?"

"Why?"

"To do something about it."

"There's nothing to do."

"I don't believe that."

"Only superpowers can hurt superpowers. Individuals can't touch them."

"The Resistance can hurt them."

"The Resistance is a superpower?" The man takes another drag on his hookah pipe.

"You bet they are. Are you Edison Blair? I've come a long way and I just want to talk to him. What happened to my father is not right. Something has to be done, and I know Edison Blair feels the same way. We can figure out something together. I know we can."

"I'm glad to see there are still optimistic people in the world. There are so few left."

"Who are all these people here? Muslims?"

"We are not Muslims. We are Kurds." Wild Hair is still standing behind him.

Sprocket looks back at Wild Hair, then back to the man in front. "I'm in a tent of Muslims. How are they going to help you get revenge?"

"Who says I want revenge?"

"I've read your stories in the Source. They're dripping with contempt and hate for the government. So I know the main 'who' already. The President's administration did in my father. What's the what, how, and the direct 'who?'"

"Your father was working on the story of the murder of the

President's campaign manager. He put all the pieces together and was about to release the story publicly. They found out about it and had him neutralized. That's it."

"That's it?"

"I begged him not to go home. I begged so hard that if I could have come through his phone and grabbed him, I would have, but he didn't see the danger. That's why I'm alive. Before Western Europe fell, I saw the danger. My friends and family didn't. That's why I'm alive and they're not."

"And you live with the people who did that to you?"

"The people I live with didn't do that and would destroy the Caliphate and release Old Britain if they could, along with all Western Europe and all the people in the Middle East who want their own Homelands."

"Oh, you're part of the 'Free Old Western Europe' movement. I only care about my bio-dad. What does 'IRA' mean anyway?"

"Islamic Reformation Army," Wild Hair says.

"Alliance," Edison Blair corrects.

"We would be an army if not for the bourgeoisie founders of the movement, who are more interested in incrementalism," Wild Hair says. "I should change my religion and join the Resistance. They know how to fight."

"Are we going to be able to talk?" Sprocket asks. "Are you Mr. Blair?"

"I am."

"Do you have any photos of my father? I have only a few."

"I have many. I'll copy them for you before you go."

"Good."

"I was hoping to work for you. I'll never be as good as him, but you can train me, mentor me. I have a lot of contacts in the Outlands and Trog-land in America. That's how I found the

Resistance. I could grow those contacts and come up with stories."

"True journalism is a dying art."

"No, it just needs to be updated. You have the platform already. You just need new people, with new angles. I can do that. All we have to do is wait."

"Wait for what?"

"Until the story comes along that we can use to topple the government, or topple the entire world order."

Edison laughs. "The media definitely can't do that anymore."

"I think it can."

"I used to think like you."

"Then I'll be the used-to-be Edison Blair."

"Will you live here then? You won't be able to stay in America."

"I was thinking of Canada. I'll live with the funny Star Trek people."

People in the tent around them laugh out loud.

"Do you know there is a secret Star Trek religious movement in the Caliphate?"

"Great! Maybe that can help you here."

"Why not live in the Russian Bloc?"

"I'd have to learn another language. I'm horrible with other languages."

"Live here in the Caliphate as I do."

"I don't think so. Pale skin. The heat. The sand."

"The real reason is you don't want to live with Muslims."

Sprocket smiles. "Well, I can't. My neck starts to itch whenever I'm around them."

People laugh again.

Sprocket turns to Mr. Wild Hair. "You have to give back my dagger when I leave. It belongs to an Arab Christian and he will come after you."

"I don't doubt it," he says. "There used to be Kurdish Christians, too. All gone now."

Sprocket turns back to Edison. "Do you know who they sent after my father? How it was done? Something exploded from his stomach, that's all I know. That's it. Then his body disappeared from the morgue."

"The killer was called 'The Man Made Out of String.'"

"Is that some kind of drone?"

"We don't know, but it was delivered by another agent," Edison says. "I found that out from…special sources I once had in the government. The other agent is called 'The Delivery Man.' They're apparently a team."

"Why hasn't anyone tried to find them?"

"We can't find them. We don't know how and they haven't been used again. Logan was probably their first and only contract."

"Are you telling me they used my father as a guinea pig for their contract kill?" Sprocket is fuming.

"That's what I believe."

"Then let's get them."

"Do you know something today that I haven't figured out in four years?"

"Not me, the Resistance. They know how, but it will take both of us."

7:41 p.m.

Sprocket has left—his journey back home will take even longer than his trip to the region.

Edison Blair reflects on his conversation and their plan. He shares his meal with Mr. Wild Hair (Kashi).

"Do you think they will find the murderers?" Kashi asks.

"The Resistance is a very determined people. You know that better than I," Edison answers.

"What about our plans? You must remember that the Middle East is not like any other part of the world. Here, blood-ties, bloodlines are very important. You and your little secret group of ex-Western Europans don't understand that. Your goals will never succeed without understanding that. What blood-ties do you have to the land you seek to re-conquer?"

"Royal blood, you mean?"

"Yes, which of your people that survived have blood-ties to that land? That would be your claim to the land, not that you once lived there. No one cares about that."

"There's the Swedish royal family that escaped. Three of them, sisters, are still alive. We think Denmark's got out too, but none of the others."

"Those would be valid claims, but I don't think any would respect countries that made laws that forced men to sit on a stool when they had to pee."

"There's also the last remaining monarch of Great Britain; changed his names many times."

"That would be better, much better. A male heir, a respected country of Old Western Europa."

"The last King of England."

"Do you know this man?"

Edison takes another slow puff from his pipe before he says, "*I am that man.*"

Kashi smiles. He always suspected there was something more to Edison. "But no heirs?"

"No."

"That is not good. You must have a wife and you must have children. That is what we will do for you. We will have our

Kurdish Homeland. You will have your English Homeland. They may be the same thing, because if you have Kurdish children, heirs, you would have your own…Muslim army."

Edison looks on with a smirk.

"Wouldn't that be ironic," Kashi says. "You were run out of your Homeland by Muslim armies, only to return one day to reclaim it with your own Muslim army."

"What you're saying, Kashi, is bloody mad."

"Allah's way often seems that way to us. He does have a sense of humor. One day."

"Yes, one day."

Intercepted Voice Transmission
12 noon, 3 April 2093

"Yes, this is Sprocket. I found Edison Blair…yeah. I can't believe they consider this guy a terrorist. He's a freedom fighter, that's what he is. I know who killed my parent, who they sent? It was a secret government operation run straight out of the White House by the President. Yeah…Logan was going to expose their killing of Lucifer Mestopheles. Yeah…the President's national campaign manager…yeah. He was going to tell this campaign manager's parents next, probably the only people on the planet who could bring down his presidency. Well, we're working on the story now. It's dynamite. The hitman is called the Man Made Out of String, that's the code name…I don't know what it means. We don't even know if it's human, but we'll find out. And here's the kicker—this hitman always works with another person…yeah…the Delivery Man. We're going to expose him, too."

Department of Homeland Defense and Intelligence Agency Security Dispatch / 3 April 2093

Notify HOMELAND that communication was intercepted by subject: Sprocket working with subject: Edison Blair, ex-citizen of Old England, immigrated to United States in 2065, now a terrorist fugitive overseas. Top-secret SCI projects MAN-STRING and DELIVERY MAN referenced.

Chapter Seven: The Delivery Man

Washington Hilton Hotel Ballroom, Washington DC (Four Years Ago)
6:30 p.m., 4 June 2089

President Wilson has not been seen in public for many months. The event is a special fundraiser for his major donors in the District. It is a tuxedo affair for the men and little black dress affair for the women.

He mingles in the crowd with his Secret Service detail close by. They move him from the VIP section of the banquet, with its one hundred major donors, to the general area, where thousands of people wait behind a partition—smiling, cheering, and reaching out their hands to greet him. He immediately walks to them. Wilson shakes hands with a large smile on his face.

A man in a red fedora extends his hand toward the President. The man is smiling, unthreatening, but instead of shaking the President's hand, he reaches in and pokes him in the center of his chest with an index finger.

"The finger of God," he says and starts to walk backward.

President Wilson is unnerved and his Secret Service detail is already calling on their ear-sets to apprehend the man. The man seems to be enveloped by the crowd. Plainclothes Secret Servicemen rush into the crowd from three sides. The man ducks into the mass of people. They can't see him. The three Secret Servicemen reach the spot and all that remains, lying on the ground, is the red fedora. The man is gone.

The lead Secret Service agent takes no chances. Secret Service surrounds the President and whisks him out of a side door to the secure parking lot and into the Presidential limousine. Agents swarm into the banquet hall to detain the entire body of attendees.

The White House, Washington, DC
12 noon, 3 April 2093

"My dear visitors, you must now consider yourselves to be members of the initiated. You must never refer to this grand tek-city as Washington, DC or even simply 'DC.' That is the language of the unsophisticated. There are forty thousand cities in America, but there is only one District." Those are the lines of Mr. District, the tek-city's self-appointed tourism czar.

President Wilson remembers the "finger of God" incident. He touches his chest, but focuses his attention back on his two division heads.

"I don't want your divisions distracted by trivialities. I don't want to hear about wormhole weapons, or imaginary bases on Mars, or anything else. Deployment! When I was Homeland Director, I wrote a report for the President and Vice President.

"We don't have enough enlisted troops to fight a three-front war, which is my mandate, and the Joint Chiefs' recommendation to simply reinstate the draft is foolish. We can't re-institute such a thing after more than a century. No one would comply, neither in the tek-cities nor the outer tek–cities. And most of them we wouldn't want in our military forces under any circumstances. We have a growing subculture, and I'm not talking about the Jew-Christians. The problem is having the bodies, the units, to fill as many military uniforms as possible.

"Do you know why I'm planning to go to this juvenile summit in Russia?" the President asks. "Because I need to see with my own eyes the tek that our enemies have. They'll show it off out of national vanity. I need to see where they are, anything we haven't gotten from our spy services. If it comes down to a man-to-man battle, we lose. No one has more people than the CHINs and the Caliphate, who since absorbing Western Europe have many more people than we do. So it comes down to superior tek."

Mr. West, a sleek man with braided silver hair, speaks first. "Sir, I want you to know that you will have all the units you need. We're calling them anthro-droids. They don't just look human; their systems are self-sustaining, self-repairing and they're virtually sentient."

The other man scoffs. "Robots can't be self-aware," Mr. Garrison says. He is a relatively small man. "I can talk to a pet and fool myself into believing that it understands me, but it doesn't."

"Sir, we have a standing robot army now," West continues. "And with the auxiliary tek from the program, we will also be able to create the latest advanced mech robot shock troops, robot-suits for our human soldiers, and create temporary cyborgs, as needed, for any military deployment."

"Mr. President, all robots are vulnerable to EMP attacks—" Garrison adds before being interrupted.

"Not these units."

"What about hack-attacks from enemy tek-heads? Use our own robot forces against us."

"That is not possible, Mr. President."

"Biologic units are the best option for any real, major war, sir."

The President verbally steps in. "Gentlemen, the purpose of Project New People is to give this country *all* options. Whether it's a robot army, cyborg army, cybernetically enhanced army,"—he turns to Garrison—"clone army or MML army, we need it all. Whether it is our successors or theirs in the future, this country must be prepared and ready for all threats, using everything we have. That is, and will always be, our primary duty to the American people."

"Everything will be kept out of the public eye until deployed by you, sir," says West.

"We will deliver all the biological units you need, sir," Mr. Garrison says.

"We're not doing anything our enemies aren't. We just have to do it better."

"Yes, Mr. President," they both say.

The Outlands, Florida
10:00 a.m., 4 April 2093

Every state in the US has them—the Outlands. The outskirts of the tek-cities are technically part of the city, but for the average tek-dweller they are not. They are the border towns, the neo-suburbs; the places where people live who don't—or can't—live in the tek-cities for whatever reason, but work in the city. The Outlands are associated with "lower" classes, Jew-Christians, or the criminal-class. It's next to the tek-cities, but not a part of it really, and it isn't the crazy Trog-lands much farther away. The buildings are not as tall, the tek is not as good, and drones are not as frequent. There is lots of underutilized space and the metro lines don't go there. The government created the tek-cities. Random people created the Outlands outside them.

The sky is very overcast today. Sprocket enters the sprawling two-story housing structure; it's spread out over two miles.

The Delivery Man arrives and exits his car. Most of the Outlands in America don't have auto-drive—these towns are not connected to the Grid—which is probably the main reason tek-dwellers don't come here (or like it); they can't get here. Tek-city dwellers don't know how to manually drive; the Grid does that.

He is a plain man, dressed in a purple office suit with a white shirt and a black hat, which is tilted down to conceal his face. In his right hand is a silver case. It doesn't take him long to get to the closest entrance of the two-story mega-complex. He casually walks up to the second level. When he reaches a secluded spot between two apartment homes, he stops to wait, reading something on his palm tablet.

10:09 a.m.

Sprocket watches the man on the vid-cam feed on his tablet while sitting in his secure room. How exactly did it happen? Did his father even see this Delivery Man? Did he see his Man Made Out of String killer? The questions race through his mind and he remembers what Edison Blair told him. *"I begged him not to go home. I begged so hard that if I could have come through his phone and grabbed him, I would have, but he didn't see the danger."* Sprocket does know the danger. He wishes he was a fighter, but he'll have to save that for a nice dream. This is the closest he will ever get; the professionals will take over from here. He gets up and disappears down the secret stairway. *Next destination: Canada—my new home.*

The Delivery Man looks back and sees two men slowly coming around the corner, talking about drugs. He hears a door open and turns back. At the other end of the hallway, a woman puts one suitcase after another into the hallway and closes the door. She grabs them and starts toward him.

The hallways are narrow. The Delivery Man stands against the wall to give her a path to pass. He glances at the two men at the other end, who continue their conversation. They notice the woman too and follow his lead by moving closer to the wall.

A musical theme starts to play. The Delivery Man tilts up his hat and touches his ear to answer his phone. "Hello."

The woman throws a suitcase at him. The sonic explosion knocks the Delivery Man up and into the wall. He falls to the ground. *The two men approach with their collapsible taser rifles and fire multiple electrical stun rounds into his body.* The contractor is down and out cold before he even knew what hit him.

A perfect take-down, they think, an easy operation. Now "grab him and bag him."

One of the men reaches for the silver case. The Delivery Man's head turns and he swings his body around to kick the man. The first man is knocked off his feet. Before the second man can shoot at him again, the Delivery Man jumps to his feet and kicks again. The second man falls backwards to the floor. The Delivery Man grabs the silver case, spins, and throws it at the woman, hitting her in the face and knocking her to the ground as she drops the gun that she was about to shoot him with.

From a door at the other end of the hallway, a third man steps out and fires at the Delivery Man with a tek-rifle. It hits the contract killer in the chest and sends him flying back through the air and crashing to the ground again. Goth Lila appears behind the third man with her own tek-rifle. They both run toward everyone.

The first man who was going to grab the silver case tries to do so again. The Delivery Man stands again. The entire center of his suit is black, but he runs at them. A gun appears in his hand and he fires once; all the lights in the hallway go out.

The team hits the ground as their optics engage—they are all wearing corneal lenses and see in both night- and infrared-vision. The hallway is dark, but they can see everything. He's gone. Lila notices an open door. Something metal hits the ground near them. Lila instinctively gets up in the dark and jumps over everyone to the front.

"Override! Shields!" All of theirs activate.

The grenade explodes and throws them back. Their "lobster-claw" shields save them—the high-tek, collapsible shields popped out from the upper back portion of their body armor.

The team throws photo-grenades and the entire hallway is instantaneously bright. The tek-rifleman fires a drone round, which re-acquires the target and flies through the open door of one of the apartments. They hear the explosion. The other three team members run to the open door and throw in multiple stun grenades. The grenades explode in rapid succession; they can hear objects inside fall, shatter, and break.

The Delivery Man is in the bedroom in the apartment and is about to jump out the window. The window shatters. He's hit in the chest again and looks outside to see four more tek-riflemen firing at him from the parking lot. Every round hits its mark. He collapses to the ground, falling on his back.

They want me alive—very unwise.

The team appears at the bedroom door with weapons aimed as they approach cautiously. One man scans the contractor's body for weapons.

"Nothing," says one of them. "He has a very faint heartbeat."

"Do you see any body armor underneath his clothes?" asks another. "I don't see anything."

Two of them reach down to shackle his hands; the other two, his legs.

"Where's that silver case?" Lila asks.

The Delivery Man sits up. He breaks his hand shackles, grabs the first tek-rifleman, and throws him violently into Lila, sending them both falling out the bedroom entrance. He grabs the other man and woman by their necks, choking them.

The remaining man takes his rifle and smashes the butt of the weapon into the contractor's face, but nothing happens. He strikes again and again, each time with more force. The Delivery Man doesn't flinch and continues choking the two people. Lila appears and fires point-blank at his arm joint, blowing out his elbow and splattering blood. Both people are released and dropped, gasping for air. The Delivery Man leaps to his feet again and, with his other arm, hits Lila and the other man, sending both of them falling back across the room.

The man who was almost choked to death grabs the Delivery Man by the neck and now chokes him with the cybernetic enhancements of his own body-armor gloves. The woman fires one electric round after another into the contractor's chest. The man notices something about the contract killer's eyes. The Delivery Man grabs the man's hands from his neck and everyone hears the bones being crushed.

"Ahhh!" the man yells as he's thrown across the room. The contractor kicks the woman back.

The Delivery Man grabs the single bed in the room with his super-strength and is about to—Lila swings her tek-rifle at the Delivery Man's head with lightning speed and uses every ounce of force her enhanced body-armor can provide. *Crack!*

Lila had extended the metal hook attachment at the tip of her rifle. With it, the tek-rifle can be used to cut, stab, or act as a hook weapon. The Delivery Man feels his head wound with the hand of his good arm; the tip of the metal hook is fully embedded in his head. He yanks it out and they all hear something snap—the hook itself. *His skin seems to be slipping from his skull. He reaches up and starts to rip off his own face—skin and dripping blood.* Lila and her team watch in shock. They see it now—*his metallic face.*

"Take it down!" Lila yells. "No more non-lethals! Deadly force!"

The other two members fire non-stop at it. The robot ignores them as it takes the tek-rifle, aims, and pulls the trigger rapidly.

"You need to be human to fire that, robot!" Lila has pulled her secondary weapon and the three of them fire.

The robot goes down again. It's not moving.

"Where's that case?" Lila yells. "Get it!"

The female team member runs out of the room. Lila looks at the wounded male team member. Actually, they're all wounded to some degree. Her body-armor is damaged in the back and arm areas, and something is cutting into her shoulder.

"Okay?" she asks.

"I'm okay," he says, but his hands are visibly crushed and bleeding.

The others arrive and the room fills with more than a dozen armed team members.

"Keep your weapons on it," Lila says. "No, in fact—"

They all begin to fire non-stop at the robot, stopping only when its body is smoldering. The smoke clears.

"There was something about his eyes," says the male team member with the crushed hands. "Something was off."

The female team member returns to the room with the case. "I got it."

Lila is about to reach for the case when the team starts firing again. She turns to see the robot on its feet again as it dives out the window. Team members run to the window and continue firing.

"Target has escaped!" she yells into her wrist-comm. "Have our drones target anything moving on the ground within the perimeter. Use localized EMP rounds. Target is a robot, I repeat, target is a combat robot."

"Done," a voice on the other end says.

Lila looks around at everyone. "Damn!"

"Lila, we'll find it," one of them says.

"We have never lost a target before—never. Why isn't it showing up on sensors?" She stares at her wrist display. "There's no movement outside." Lila runs to the window to look out.

In the sky is the robot—floating away on a single balloon coming out of its head. There is a head, its "good" arm, and multiple spine-like attachments from its neck; the rest of its body is gone. Whether the damage to those body parts was too severe, or with them it would be too heavy to escape, all its body parts will have to be found too. Her optics zoom in on its face. The robot's eyes must have done the same. It smiles at her, cocks its hand like a gun, and pretends to shoot her. It then waves good-bye.

Lila clenches her teeth in anger—*robot bastard.* "It's outside in the air!" She runs from the window, but stops when she sees that her team is about to open the case. "How many times did we scan that?"

"Multiple times, all frequencies."

"We scanned him too, but didn't detect that it was a robot." She speaks into her wrist-comm. "The robot is in the air. It's flying away eastward on a balloon. Shoot it down!" She looks at the case again. They all look at each other; everyone is thinking the same thing.

The "walker" enters the room. The thin robot surrogate approaches the silver suitcase. Its hands are bio-sim tek—they not only look like human hands, but have the same temperature as real ones with a real pulse.

Boom! The explosion destroys the entire section of the two-story complex. Other parts of the building begin to collapse like falling dominoes.

Lila and her team look at each other. They watch from an elevated point, a quarter mile away. A SUV drives up with more of the team.

"Nothing," the driver says, shaking his head. "No balloon and nothing on the ground or in the air."

"It was flying away on a balloon! How fast could it go?"

Another team member says, "Lila, we have to go now. Grid drones will be here any minute."

She shakes her head in disgust. They must leave immediately.

The robot got away.

Continuum Meeting, Secret Location
10:00 p.m., 4 April 2093

Lila is doing the debriefing. What went wrong? Everyone is standing for the hastily put-together meeting in the darkened room. Pictures of the Delivery Man are on the wall vid-screen—before and after he ripped off his face.

"It wasn't a surrogate. It was autonomous and nothing external was controlling it," she says.

"Please explain the technical designations again for me," says one of the members.

"An android looks like a person, externally. A sim-droid is a robot made to look like a person externally and internally. We have them ourselves in our medical training schools. But ours are made to mimic life for study, not for anything else. This one was made for combat purposes. It was intelligent and adaptive. *I believe that it could think.*"

"Think?" asks a female Continuum member.

"It tried to trick us. Made us think an item was important when the only purpose of that item was to kill all of us. It knew we had set a trap for it. It even knew to use a non-tek way to escape from us. The bomb wasn't only to kill us, but to destroy its personal vehicle too, and to deprive us of any possible intel from it. Mr. Robot got away using a balloon. We used that method ourselves. We still don't know how it fooled our sensors; they showed biological readings."

M is among the attendees. She has a thought. "Maybe you're over-thinking it and your scanners weren't fooled. We've been thinking that this Man Made Out of String is a code name. Maybe it's more literal. Maybe the Delivery Man is the delivery mechanism."

"The Man Made Out of String is inside and that's what our scanners were reading?"

"Yes, and since we know now that the silver case was, in fact, a decoy, maybe its purpose was always to be a fail-safe weapon; not to destroy a captor primarily, but to ensure that a captor would never be able to capture it, either of them. It simply improvised for this situation."

"This was more—more than advanced adaptive and improvisational artificial intelligence. It gloated. It was gloating as it escaped from us. It was like real human emotions."

"It's not human so its emotions can't be human—only an illusion."

"Maybe, M," one of the male Continuum members says, "they have created a true quantum-brain robot, not like all the quasiquants they have in use. They've been working on it for decades. They want to turn humans into killing machines and give killing machines emotions."

"But use such tek as a hitman?" asks someone else.

"Why not?" someone else adds. "It's something they would do."

Lila sighs. "The fact is we failed. I let it get away."

"You didn't fail," M says. "We know what it is now and we know what to look for."

"If they have one, they have many more. Also, the government has lifted the ban on robotic self-replication in the commercial industry."

"Which means they have already done so for the military and intel industry."

"If we could have just gotten our hands on that tek…" Lila could kick herself.

"You got the intel we needed. Others will take over from here. This Delivery Man will see us again."

"I still feel I failed."

"Lila, don't think that," M says. "The mission wasn't the Delivery Man. The mission was the Man Made Out of String. We know a lot more now than we did before. The Delivery Man is an added bonus. And Lila, we have thinking robots, too."

"The Cube," Secret Location
8:32 a.m., 5 April 2093

Mr. West tours the underground facility with his staff. They are sitting in an open-air flying-saucer-type hovercraft to survey the "warehouse." Robot arms make humanoid robots, one after another, on an assembly line. The room is filled from ground to ceiling with the units.

They leave the hovercraft and take the moving walkway back to executive offices. One of his deputies is waiting at the elevators with a man and woman he's never seen before.

A century ago, religious Americans named things of science after Greek and Roman gods. Today, Pagans name their machines from, as they would say, Jew-Christian mythology.

"Sir, you wanted to see Adam and Eve before you left."

West looks at the anthro-droids and grabs each of their wrists. "I can feel a pulse and warmth. We really can make them."

"We didn't make them, sir. Our robots did." She smiles. "They can make them look like any living thing in the world."

West is pleased, but he notices his chief security agent's face. "What?"

"We had a breach yesterday, sir. Unauthorized people may have seen one of our independent models. We were informed only this morning."

"*Independent models*? What independent models? No unit is allowed out of my facility without my authorization."

"Special Services out of the White House commissioned some units for domestic and international operations recently."

"You mean black operations? This is unconscionable. I shut down that interference four years ago. The unauthorized personnel were whom exactly?"

"They may have been domestic terrorists." West's mouth hangs open as he listens. "Sir, they wouldn't have even known what they saw, if they saw anything at all."

"We have an ultra-top-secret program and we allow *terrorists* to see them?"

"They wouldn't have known what they saw, sir."

"Please tell me they weren't the Jew-Christian ones?"

The chief agent thinks for a moment. "They were, sir, but…what does that matter?"

"*The sim-droid program was inspired by them!* All this 'Jew-Christians are Trogs' is all propaganda. None of it is true. Letting them see them is like announcing, at the top of our lungs that we have dramatically upgraded our robotic forces. They'll do the same and they will not be foolish enough to show us what they come up with. Get me Special Services on the phone! We will cease all the black ops bullcrap with my robots. I'll speak with the President again if I have to. Wait…which program was it? What was compromised exactly?"

"There are hundreds of them, sir. It will take time to find out, but I will call now."

"It was probably the Delivery Man program, sir," another agent says.

West is speechless again. "That's our joint-op with Garrison on the New People Project. This is…worse. Not one ultra-top-secret program compromised, but both, both our robotics and genetics warfare programs." West is in a state of near-panic. "I need the President on the phone, now! This is a priority, an emergency…urgent! And find me Garrison, too. Where is he? He couldn't have allowed this to happen on purpose. Where is he?"

"He is with the Homeland Director at the Lagoon, sir."

"He's with whom at the Lagoon?" West's face is red.

"An unscheduled tour; it was last minute, sir."

"The White House has never sent her here, to the Cube. Why is she there?"

"We don't know, sir."

"This is politics again, all of it. They don't respect us, this constant organic bigotry against the synthetic. All of us are robots in a way—you, me, all humankind. The human body is an organic machine. We're just using metal for flesh. My Program must be respected. It may be the savior of this country one day. Instead they send the Homeland Director, not here to the Cube to see our progress and accomplishments, but to Monster Lagoon to see the *freak show.*"

The After Eden Series: Tek-Fall concludes in Episode II, *Hell's Menagerie*.

REFERENCES

Sprocket is also in *Thy Kingdom Fall (After Eden Series, Book #1)*.

The mentioned **Logan** is in *Thy Kingdom Fall (After Eden Series, Book #1)*.

Goth Lila is also in *Thy Kingdom Fall (After Eden Series, Book #1)* and the beginning of *Stars and Scorpions (After Eden Series, Book #2)*.

The mentioned **Goli** is also in *Thy Kingdom Fall (After Eden Series, Book #1)* and *Stars and Scorpions (After Eden Series, Book #2)*.

Edison Blair and **Bunny** are also in *Thy Kingdom Fall (After Eden Series, Book #1)*.

Haggard and the **League of Artifacts, Curios, Curiosities, Mementos, Relics, and Antiquities** are also in *Stars and Scorpions (After Eden Series, Book #2)*.

M and her husband **"General" Moses** are also in *Thy Kingdom*

Fall (After Eden Series, Book #1).

Kristiana and the **Amish** are also in *Thy Kingdom Fall (After Eden Series, Book #1).*

The **Resistance** and **Continuum** are introduced in *Thy Kingdom Fall (After Eden Series, Book #1).*

The **African Collective** is discussed in *Stars and Scorpions (After Eden Series, Book #2)* and fully shown in *Hell's Menagerie (After Eden Series: Tek-Fall, Episode II).*

The mentioned **Magi** are in *Thy Kingdom Fall (After Eden Series, Book #1), Rising Leviathan (After Eden Series, Book #3),* and *Red Halo (After Eden Series, Book #4).*

The mentioned **Shogun** are in *Rising Leviathan (After Eden Series, Book #3)* and *Red Halo (After Eden Series, Book #4).*

President T. Wilson is also in *Thy Kingdom Fall (After Eden Series, Book #1)* and *Rising Leviathan (After Eden Series, Book #3).*

The Man Made Out of String is introduced in *Thy Kingdom Fall (After Eden Series, Book #1).*

Project New People is introduced in *Stars and Scorpions (After Eden Series, Book #2).*

The mentioned world summit is in *Rising Leviathan (After Eden Series, Book #3).*

HELL'S MENAGERIE

THE AFTER EDEN SERIES: TEK-FALL
EPISODE II

A Hell's Menagerie Poem

God creates Animals.
God creates Man.
God tells Man to take care of the Animals.
Man exterminates the Animals.
Man creates New-Animals.
New-Animals kill Man.
New-Animals kill each other.
God resets the universe.

The following story takes place *after* the events of

Thy Kingdom Fall (After Eden Series, Book #1) and

Stars and Scorpions (After Eden Series, Book #2)

and *before* the events of

Rising Leviathan (After Eden Series, Book #3)

Prologue

**The Outlands, Florida
10 a.m., 4 April 2093**

The Delivery Man arrives and exits his car. Most of the Outlands in America don't have auto-drive—these towns are not connected to the Grid—which is probably the main reason tek-dwellers don't come here (or like it); they can't get here. Tek-city dwellers don't know how to manually drive; the Grid does that.

He is a plain man, dressed in a purple office suit with a white shirt. His black hat is tilted down to conceal his face. In his right hand is a silver case. It doesn't take him long to get to the closest entrance of the two-story building mega-complex. He casually walks up to the second level—*right into the trap*.

But it is the Delivery Man—an android like they have never seen before—that almost kills them all.

In the sky is the robot—floating away on a single balloon coming out of its head. There is a head, its "good" arm, and multiple spine-like attachments from its neck; the rest of its body is gone. It smiles at the female Continuum member watching it, cocks its hand like a gun, and pretends to shoot her. It then waves good-bye as it disappears from view.

Continuum Meeting, Secret Location
10 p.m., 4 April 2093

Over thirty years ago Faithers began abandoning the tek-cities of America to live apart, far from the Pagan majority populations. Today, there exist two separate and distinct Americas—the atheistic Tek World and, beyond even the Outlands and Trog-land territories, the Faith World. Anti-religious government laws and leaders may have caused the Separatist Movement, but it would have happened anyway due to the persecution, surveillance, and ever-expanding intrusion into daily life. Now even the Pagans were dividing into those who lived in the tek-cities and those anarchistic sub-populations that didn't.

Faithers left the general society, then created their own—their own government, infrastructure, security services, civilian military, and intelligence services. The Continuum.

"This was more…much more than advanced adaptive or improvisational artificial intelligence. It gloated. It was gloating as it escaped from us. It was like real human emotions." Goth Lila gives her debrief of the encounter. Unlike the other, more conservatively dressed Christians in the room, she is all in black, like any Goth would be— spiky, jet-black hair, three ear piercings in each earlobe, black eyeliner, and three-ring necklaces.

"You got the intel we needed," M says to her. "Others will take over from here. This Delivery Man will see us again." M is an older woman with dark brown skin and exotic green eyes. She has a unique hairdo of large curls no longer than four inches. She is dressed casually in a long-sleeved white dress.

"I still feel I failed."

"Lila, don't think that," M reassures. "The mission wasn't the Delivery Man. The mission was the Man Made Out of String. We know a lot more now than we did before. The Delivery Man is an added bonus. And Lila, we have thinking robots too."

Lila reflects on this revelation. "I hope ours are better than this android thing."

M only smiles. "We've done our part. I'll get the Continuum's authorization to move Project Tek-Fall to the next phase."

Cyberspace
Continuum Meeting / 5 April 2093

There is darkness. A lone flashing green dot appears first, then dozens, hundreds of thousands, millions, and then billions and more. The secret holographic virtual meeting in Freespace—the corner of the Net not created, run, or monitored by governments—begins. The code becomes a room, and in the room several people stand in a circle. Half of the holo-identities are green, and half are red. One of the male figures is glowing as he talks.

"But what is the exact threat to the Continuum," he asks, "to escalate so dramatically?"

Another figure glows. It is M. She answers, "Now we know that Project New People of Galerius's Grid government is *both* its mechanized and bio-warfare divisions—tactical robotics, cybernetic human and animal soldiers, weaponized clones, post-natal bio-engineered soldiers, neonatal genetically engineered soldiers."

The first figure glows again. "All of that is very frightening and, yes, the Pagans are playing at their own perverted version of 'god,' but disturbing as all that is, they're doing what all nations do—global war preparations, stockpiles, weapon systems, war games, building up their armed camps all over the world. But we are not their focus anymore. One could argue that they've switched their persecution to the anarchistic subcultures of Pagans right outside their own tek-cities."

"We agree that the concern is not the growing war apparatus of America, or the CHINs, or any other superpower," M says. "We know what they are doing. But the Continuum isn't a collection of domestic organizations anymore. We're global too, and we continue to stretch our reach. The real concern is the myriad of rogue elements around the world that are neither under the control of any government nor under even the most basic of surveillance. It is these rogue elements that pose an immediate and direct threat to the completion of our own critical projects, including Behemoth and Leviathan."

"What is the worst-case scenario?"

"Remote regions are becoming their living laboratories, and we fear the likely and radical alteration of these regions by invasive robotic and biological contamination. With no governments in these regions, there are no biohazard countermeasures of any kind and no tek-jammer systems to naturally prevent such an eventuality. These regional ecosystems outside Tek World, the Outlands and beyond, are threatened. We operate in that 'beyond.' Our primary operations are moving more and more into that 'beyond.' If that 'beyond' is threatened, then we're threatened. These rogue elements also have endless financial means to bribe the right officials, where there might be any government to monitor them."

"The proponents of this course of action, this escalation, would have us divert our precious, limited resources away from our ultimate projects to this global…seek and destroy operation?"

"But it's no longer theory. Quasi-sentient mechanical and man-made bio-organisms have been created. They will replicate, reproduce, and spread. This cannot be allowed to happen, especially when these creations should never be allowed to exist, not now or ever, or at least until we're done. So the answer to your question is yes."

"Could our data and projections be wrong? Everyone in this room has lived through supposed claims by authorities to get the people to do one thing or another, only to find out that the data was wrong. Just because we are the authorities now in our own world doesn't mean that we should be any less skeptical."

"I believe skepticism to be an unwritten Commandment. I draw everyone's attention to the appendix x-file for review from the Magi Order. It includes images of actual specimens captured and salvaged by our agents in the field, most notably in Russian Bloc, CHIN, and Asian Consortium territories. Everyone is already familiar with the specimens from the Day of the Scorpions event in Mexico."

Everyone's holo-identities flicker and go out of phase for a moment. The images return after a few minutes.

"My God, they're doing it. They're making their own hellish menageries."

Another figure glows. "But wouldn't the Continuum, in actuality, be *protecting* Tek World? The same Tek World that's been the mortal threat to every Faither man, woman, and child alive?"

"Please know the operation would only indirectly help Tek World. It directly helps us."

"Do we think the op would be successful?"

"We do. Project Tek-Fall will succeed in the objectives designated."

The holo-identities freeze for a few moments, then return to normal stream. The reds change to green.

M continues. "An American bio-scientist known as 'The Keeper,' who disappeared back in March of 2090, must be found. She is the visionary 'mother' of these bio-scientists. She invented the procedures that are the foundation of all their work. She trained most of them, regardless of what governments they work for currently. She personally knows all of them—every scientist, theorist, and financier. Decimating these rogue elements must become every bit the priority as the completion of our ultimate projects. Every region in our territories of operation must be protected from every manner of mechanical, biological, and hybrid monster they can create."

Continuum Directive Update / 1 October 2093

Newly acquired intel suggests acquisition of The Keeper is more probable via an American bio-scientist known as 'Frankenstein Girl.'

Chapter One: Hell Boys

"I saw Joseph Stalin shoot Che Guevara dead and then proceed to beat Pol Pot to death. Mao Zedong and Adolf Hitler sat there laughing. It was all an epic achievement of science!"

The Facility, Secret Location
2:32 p.m., 6 March 2090

Uncle Joe killed his brothers, Che and Pol, because he felt that they had not killed enough people to be part of their *Billion Dead Club*. He was genuinely offended by their existence.

That was the catalyst. It began as a tiny whisper of a voice in her head and had grown into unsettling screams of conscience. They were sim-clones—not the actual murderous despots, not even real clones of the actual murderous despots—but everyone treated them as if they were the real thing. More importantly, the Hell Boys *believed* they were the real men.

The Keeper decided one day that she would kill all her Boys. This spontaneous morality that mirrored, what she often said aloud, "the archaic and simple-minded, paleo-religious social constructs" of Jew-Christians had first crept into her mind more than a year ago. She fought it within herself intensely at the beginning and wondered how such an upstanding, free-thinking Pagan scientist as herself could have anything in common with *those* people. But over the course of a year, she slowly embraced her new state of mind. She became as convinced of the need to destroy them as she was to have them 'birthed' in the first place. She even announced her decision to her biological father and boss before…

"We are here to protect America," he had told her just this morning. "Give it all the weapons needed to protect itself from all foreign enemies. Science has always been the tip of this war effort. The Project is that and more. What is offensive to me is that my own offspring is now developing misgivings about work she's done without any trepidations her entire life. I am ashamed of you. You are a walking disgrace to the scientific community. You know how many scientists in the world would kill to be part of this project, if they knew of it, and you were handed the opportunity on a silver plate; the chance to be immortal, to have all speak your name. Scientists will be at the forefront of war, not passing afterthoughts as in the past."

She looked nothing like her bio-dad, with her short, grayish-blond hair and naturally fair complexion. His skin had an artificial quality—he had a full facial skin replacement, a common procedure to be 'young again,' and a well-groomed mustache and beard.

"This is freakishness and not anything noble you would pretend it to be," she said to him.

"Nobility? I have no opinion on that concept. We are ensuring the peace."

"Yes, Father dearest."

"Please stop using that bigoted, backwards term. Mother, father—I am your guardian, but that has zero relevance here." He glares at her. "You will do your work as I direct, or there will be consequences."

"Yes, you would probably need to kill me since I know too much."

"I would, without hesitation, without emotion. Any defective or inferior biological should be terminated."

"I have decided. I'm going to kill all three of them."

"I'll kill all of your children in the Zoo if you ever say that again."

Only a mother is allowed to kill her children, she thought.

Before she left the lab, she had her 'pet' kill him.

She has called this ultra-secret, underground 'black' facility home for many years, and it's so vast that it is its own independent, self-contained city. All the project scientists permanently live here, as she does. It is a network of endless sections and levels, including personnel residences, laboratories, observation rooms, waste and disposal, entertainment, cafeteria and food creation, motor pool, communications, security, and the Zoo—where the 'subjects' are kept.

Security includes *watching-walls* (every inch of its surface a surveillance-cam), robotic guards, and segregated bio-metric restricted areas. But she has already disabled all security on this level, even turning off the main hallway lights. She silently walks down the hallway, the back-up lights barely illuminating it with a creepy red glow. Or is it unsettling in her mind only because of what she is about to do?

Joseph Stalin may be wearing red clothes, but that does not hide the blood as it spills from his body. He flails around on the floor, desperately applying pressure to his deadly neck wound, but it is in vain.

Her face is splattered with some of his blood and so are her white clothes as she runs to the elevator, holding her forearm. He got her—he was so strong that he managed to slash her with her own laser knife. The elevator door opens and she lunges at Mao before he can react. She stabs Mao Zedong violently, rapidly, like an emotionless machine. *He laughs.* The monster laughs at her and she stops. He continues to laugh even as he slowly sits on the elevator floor.

"My worshipers will bring me back. You will be among my first million victims," he manages to say.

His sickening laugh begins again. She has to get out of the elevator as a wave of claustrophobia overcomes her. She backs out of the elevator and the laughing becomes gurgling before it stops and the sick smile on his face disappears as he succumbs to his wounds.

All she sees is the blood. There is a familiar smell of aftershave—

The ax misses her body by only inches, slamming into the edge of the elevator opening. How she managed to dodge it, she does not know. Adolf Hitler pulls the ax back to swing again. She kicks him with all her might. He stumbles back but manages not to fall.

"I've survived all my many assassins and I shall survive you!" he yells as he starts forward again. "There were more than two dozen. Oster and Beck. Von Stauffenberg and Von Tresckow, even celebrity traitors like Rommel, the SS, and entire armies. No one remembers any of them. But I remain immortal, only me!" The ax is raised above his head. "You can't kill a god in this world!"

He was created to be, visually, an exact 'twin' of the original, a simulated clone or sim-clone. But he believes with every brain cell that he is Adolf Hitler. They have conditioned him to believe nothing else. All the Hell Boys were conditioned to believe themselves to be who they saw in the mirror looking back at them.

Megalomaniacs are all the same, she thinks to herself, whether from nature or from a lab. His hubris is his undoing. He was *enhanced* neonatally and could have killed her easily without any external weapon, but he chose to be hands-on.

"But I am *your* god and gods know how to kill their creations." She fires her concealed wrist weapon.

His psychotic scream echoes throughout the hallway, throughout the entire level. He grips the ax handle so forcefully that he breaks it. Before her eyes, the center of his torso disintegrates, forming a disgusting hole in his body that a soccer ball could be kicked through. He collapses to the ground, dead.

She leans against the wall—it's over.

After a minute or two of staring at his remains, she moves. She retrieves the final device from one of the storage lockers. She had smuggled it in, piece by piece, over a period of many months, along with many white gallon containers. Methodically, she soaks the bodies with the fuel, each one—Joe first, Mao second, and the biomass of Adolf third. One white container after another, she pours out on the hallway floors. She throws the last container on the ground and gives her *home* a final look. This is how Klara, the only person she was close enough to call a friend, was killed, way back in 2080. *It was her*, The Keeper realizes. Klara was the catalyst of her *morality*. Klara had tried to kill Adolf at his birth.

It is funny how such defining moments in life can be so completely hidden by your own mind, she says to herself.

They will, of course, create another Menagerie, but not with this genetic material. She escapes the Facility this day, today, 6 March 2090, and it is the last day that she—The Keeper—is ever seen in public again. The other 'gods' will hunt her now and they will never stop.

Then there is the man in white with the wings etched on the back of his jacket, and the woman in black with the top hat. The mysterious couple—Jew-Christians probably—that can bend reality, alter perception, and make people vanish into oblivion, never to be seen again. They have always scared her for some reason. The rumors about the duo have become an urban legend among the internationalist bio-scientist and rogue tek-lord communities—except she knows that the myth is all too real. She's comforted by the fact that she has this fear of them, unlike many unfortunate colleagues before her, because it means they will never find her.

The bombs explode with the telltale white flames of hi-ox fuel accelerant destroying everything on the entire level. The Zoo is no more.

This Zoo is no more.

Chapter Two: Frankenstein Girl and Mona Lisa

Trog-land Territories, Colorado
10:42 p.m., 22 December 2095

A lone Doctor Mary sits inside her pod-car in the darkness, scanning the open wasteland. Pure night is unnerving to any average tek-dweller like herself. In the tek-cities, the lights are always on. Who would have thought you could see the stars with the naked eye? But this isn't one of the main tek-cities, and any place outside of them is considered 'nowhere.' For her, the only illumination is the faint glow from the stars above and, more prominently, the distant flashing lights of her destination—a Trog-land town five miles away.

In some ways, modern-day geographical hierarchy has replaced social class. Major tek-cities are the center of the universe. The retro-tek Outlands are the outskirts of the tek-cities and technically separate. They are the border towns, the neo-suburbs; the places where people live who don't—or can't—live in the tek-cities for whatever reason, but may work in the city. The Outlands are associated with lower classes, Jew-Christians, and the criminal-class. The government created the tek-cities. Random people created the Outlands outside of them.

But beyond the Outlands, for the average tek-dweller regarding Trog-land, there is only one word that comes to mind—dangerous. Random beatings, rape, and murder are all common, as well as spontaneous suicide. Anarchists and Nihilists are the worst, but there are also the pleasure-all-the-time Hedonists, drugs-all-the-time Drug Zombies, mentally unstable Space Cadets, and the like. Trog-land is where you go for the products and services that are illegal even in the general Tek World. There are no drones patrolling from the air. The police never go there, and neither do the ambulances; but cadaver wagons are plentiful. It is here where Mary's criminal career will begin.

Because of the control helmet on her head, she is oblivious to the howling winds and the pack of sickly, feral dogs nearby. Her attention is focused on her surrogate as it walks into town. Thanks to modern tek, it is the literal extension of her, but she still must be careful.

She met The Keeper only once in her life, but so many people believed they were co-conspirators. Some even started rumors of them being biological sisters. The suspicions were not unexpected, as Mary was present when some Jew-Christian, possibly a terrorist, breached the site just days after The Keeper's day of mayhem. But Mary was cleared by Homeland Security of any complicity, as were all her colleagues. It's fortunate she didn't lose her job. Otherwise, she wouldn't have any government secrets to sell.

The loudest place in the Trog-land town is the four-story Arena with its flashing structure lights and photo-drones buzzing around, keeping their lights trained on the combatants in the main ring. Three men savagely beat one another to the sounds of thousands of people yelling, screaming, and booing as they look on from the circling stands, one row higher than the one before it. The Ancient Romans used to pit men against men and men against animals; it's what the people wanted. The tek-cities allow only rule-burdened civilian fight-clubs and professional mixed martial arts matches. In the Outlands there are some good dogfights. Here, people require more raw entertainment. Even the violent robots-only, mixed martial arts competitions of Neo-Japan known as *Domu!* won't do. The only animals in this no-holds-barred fight club are the human kind—surgically enhanced with glowing eyes, razor-fang teeth, and clawed nails. If the fans are lucky, they'll get one cyborg against another or 'total chaos'—dozens of men fighting one another—all at once. Robots can't die; people can. It is one of the few places in society where premodern gender roles still hold. No biological females here. She watches through the robot's eyes as the largest man in the arena pulls a blade from his belt and starts hacking away at the other two.

The Arena is extremely popular, but the Dome is more so. Eden's Pleasure Dome is like so many others in Trog-land territories across America's fifty-three states—many even have the same name. It is literally a dome building with a large first-floor bar and dancing club, with multicolored drug clouds of psychogenic, hallucinogenic, and stimulagenic drug vapors from the drug dens on the next levels, and sex dens are on the top penthouse floors. She can see all kinds of male, female, she-male, male-she, and dual-gender hermaphrodite sex workers waving from balconies. What little clothes they have on are bright and flashing.

"Welcome to Eden," the man says. "I am Mr. Bliss. I am here to provide whatever services to make your existence as pleasurable as possible for as long as the universe will allow. Everyone is welcome in Eden—organic or synthetic."

Does Mr. Bliss know that there is synthetic organic too?

"Thank you," her robot-self replies.

The establishment *appears* clean and spotless, with tiny robots everywhere, always sweeping, dusting, and wiping up messes—vomit, blood, bodily waste, and sexual fluids—but there is no such thing as clean in Trog-land.

However, all that is ignored by the flocking masses. The primary purpose of Trog-land is pleasure. Nothing is bad, illegal, or deviant here so long as the proper units of digi-cash are exchanged between parties.

"How may I be your slave?" He looks directly at her.

Mr. Bliss struts forward a step on his black platform boots. He doesn't have an ounce of fat on his body, but he is not morbidly thin in his silvery, skintight jumpsuit with a short black cape. His long silver hair is perpetually blowing from a mini-fan device on his right shoulder. Standing behind him on either side are huge, topless men—all standing as a unit to block entrance to the Dome. Permission to enter comes from Mr. Bliss alone.

"I'm here for the Transporter," she says to him.

He studies her more closely. Surrogates are robots remotely synced to people who control the machines by their own body movements and commands. In tek-cities, robots of any kind—humanoid or pet—haven't been allowed outside the home in decades. Only the government can deploy robots in public. But here robots are plentiful. Hers is a lean, black robot with a simple faceplate head and simulated eyes and mouth. The sleeveless blue dress is the only clothing on her.

"Name?" Mr. Bliss asks as he touches his face with one of his dual cybernetic hands.

"Miss Mary." The robot's mouth doesn't physically move as it transmits her voice.

He speaks into his virtual microphone—a receiver-amplifier on his ear-set and pointing to his mouth—that also prevents anyone from hearing his words. He listens to someone speaking to him— she can tell from the fact that his ear-set is glowing yellow. The conversation draws out and he communicates to his bodyguards with hand gestures, signaling whether or not to allow in visitors.

While waiting, she looks around the Trog-town through the robot's eyes. Most tek-city dwellers will never enter the urban chaos and anarchy of Trog-land. They send others or, in this case, use surrogates to conduct their business. Even most taxis from the Outlands won't come here. Besides the pulsating beats of retro-techno music from inside the pleasure dome's first floor, she can hear screaming, yelling, and other sounds from the above floors. So much narcotic drug vapor is in the air that most people have a perpetual buzz.

His ear-set disconnects. "They are ready for you," he says.

Three large men dressed in grungy black, gray, and brown outfits scan her from head to toe with a hand device. The private room is on the first floor, and the music from the outside club is so loud that every beat rattles the walls.

"Do you have the money?" one of the men asks.

"I do."

"Then give it here. All of it."

"The agreement was half now and half later."

"We're altering the agreement. All now or else," the man says. "People get killed here every day in Trog-land. By the tenets of Darwin-god, only the strong live to the next day."

"Or the clever ones," she interjects.

The man grins. "Yeah, you're right. Do you think because you're using a surrogate that we can't track you? Tek-city people always think they're smarter than Trogs. All we have to do is scan for lone vehicles anywhere outside the town. We know every surrogate on the market and yours… has a range of four, five miles?" He flexes his arms and his cybernetically enhanced jacket flexes too. "What will it be? All the money now or do we come find you?"

"Can any one of you by yourself, without the other two, transport me to where I need to go?"

The men start to laugh. "Yes, each one of us is as smart as the other," answers the man. "Why? Are you planning to kill two of us so the remaining one does whatever you say?"

One of the men raises his arm and a collapsible tek-rifle pops out and extends. He points the weapon at her. "Three seconds! Or I'll blast your robot to the off and dead setting."

"No need." The robot surrogate straightens up and the top of its head flashes red. "Self-destructive mode has been activated." The voice is not hers but the robot's internal system one.

"You don't frighten us, female," one of the men says with a sneer.

The robot stands motionless, but the red flashing increases in frequency.

"Stop the countdown. Give us a better deal then."

The flashing stops and the robot's head swivels to look at him.

The man says, "Finding real transporters is not as easy as I think you've already experienced. What's your better deal? We just want money. And stop trying to be clever."

"Agreed."

The men relax and the armed one lowers his rifle.

"Will you honor our original agreement, then?" she asks.

"No. It's impossible to get you there so fast, and the secrecy of the flight can't be guaranteed. And you didn't tell us that you were a scientist under Homeland Security. Did you think we wouldn't check up on you? You're going to have to pay a lot more to pop you in and out of the country."

"Why didn't you say so? I will add a bonus if you can get me there by tomorrow without detection."

"How much of a bonus?"

"Every hour sooner that you get me there ahead of the original seventy-two hours, I will add ten percent of the remaining half."

"Ten percent of the total."

"Done."

"Then we leave right now."

"Don't I need to pay you?"

"Pay us when you see us."

"No, wait!" The robot lifts its open hands to shield itself.

The man blasts the robot surrogate with a high charge from his electric gun. The machine shakes, short-circuits, and collapses.

One man grabs the robot while the other man opens the room's garbage chute compartment on the wall. They throw it in and the compartment closes.

The third man touches his ear-set. "Frankenstein girl will be there tomorrow."

Dr. Mary removes her controller (helmet) as she sees a vehicle rapidly approaching with its triple high beams aimed directly at her pod-car. The dirt cloud from the vehicle blows away and a man exits. She gets out of her own car—short brown hair, a one-piece casual suit, and a furious look on her face.

"Why was my robot destroyed? I was fond of that robot. It was an expensive graduation present that I was planning on using for a long time."

The man walks to her, holding something in his hand. Her eyes narrow, trying to figure out what it is. He hands her a palm tablet.

She takes it slowly. "Why are you giving me this?"

He doesn't answer as she looks at the display. It is a wave-link recording—the ubiquitous and invisible world of electromagnetic communications and connections made visible with the device.

The man speaks now. "You can see the secure link from the surrogate to your controller." He points to the screen. "And a second one to your surrogate, and a third one, and a fourth and fifth. Your little robot was nothing but a party line. *Everybody* was watching and listening."

"That's impossible. It has Homeland security firewalls."

"And? Any system can be hacked into, even the US Grid government. Should we wait here to see who the hackers were so we can meet them and exchange niceties?"

She looks into the darkness of the wasteland toward the nearest tek-city, scanning for any sign of an approaching vehicle, drone, or aircraft. "No, we should leave immediately."

"Not as clever as you thought, huh?"

"If you knew my surrogate was hacked, why did you continue the meeting?"

"We didn't say anything critical and besides, we like to know everyone we're involved with. We don't like uninvited intruders into our business. We'll go, but we'll leave some friends here to wait for them and exchange niceties for us. No one will think anything of it. People die and disappear every day in Trog-land."

She shakes her head. "The criminal world."

"What were you expecting? The criminal world is criminal. Let's go. We'll take your pod car off your hands, too. The cost of doing business." He gestures for her to walk away from it. "And you'll be able to get yourself a replacement robot. You're going to be a rich criminal."

"Please just get me to Hong Kong light-speed fast."

"Whatever you say."

H.K. Shangri-La, Hong Kong, Chinese-Indian Alliance (CHIN) Territory
12:58 p.m., 23 December 2095

Hong Kong, often simply called HK, remains one of the top ten tek-cities in the world and the 'Jewel of Asia.' They say the closer you get to Japan from Asia, the more robotic animals, robotic pets, humanoid robots, and cyborgs there are. All tek-cities never sleep, but Hong Kong prides itself on never being the same. Every day the city's Grid changes something: the colors of the ever-flashing lights, the textures of walls, the style of lettering of digital signs, the surveillance drones from flying unicorns to pink giraffes. Long gone are any visual references to China, old Hong Kong, former British influences, or religiosity of any kind—Big Buddha and ancient temples of Buddhism, Taoism, and Confucianism are no more. No religion is illegal—unlike in America, the Supreme Islamic Caliphate, and CHIN territories—but the only 'God' here is the free market. Like Japan, it is obsessed with 'newness' and tek.

Mona Lisa casually sits, waiting. She is a stunningly beautiful woman with olive skin and silky black hair styled to hang to the right side of her face. She is wearing a neon-orange one-piece sleeveless dress, with matching pearls around her neck. She glances at a flock of brightly colored peacocks flying above, prominently covered in red, orange, and purple feathers. There's no end to the robotic wildlife in this tek-city. Her translucent gel chair and table are almost invisible, and she looks like she is sitting on thin air with her glass hovering next to her with its straw. There is no one else on the hotel's penthouse terrace; she reserved the entire space for the half-day. Even here on the one-hundredth floor, commercial drones are visible, advertising a wide array of products, almost all of them with vids of partially or fully naked men and women— human, cyborg, and robot.

She hears a chirping sound from the main penthouse elevators, which open. An immaculately dressed little man exits, wearing a silver suit with a white shirt and matching tie. He has Asiatic features, jet-black hair, and a goatee. His two large cyborg guards wearing dark glasses step out after him. Both of them have at the least robotic hands, most likely their entire arms. In this region, people like to show off their cyborgism.

"Good afternoon, Señor Tai," Mona Lisa says to the little man as they reach her. She rises temporarily from her chair.

He appreciates the courtesy. "Enchanté, Mademoiselle Gustavo."

Common among the wealthy class in this region of Asia is the practice of Franglish—speaking French with English—as well as mixing French with Cantonese, HK's official language. Strange, since the French who managed to escape the Fall of Western Europe went mostly to Australia and none have ever reciprocated by learning or teaching their offspring any Asiatic languages.

"Join me," she says.

He nods and pulls out the facing chair at the virtually invisible table. Tai relaxes in the chair and gestures his bodyguards away. "How do you like our enchanting HK?"

She watches his men return to the elevator entrance and stand on either side to face them.

"It is very nice."

"We are the gem of the Asiatic world." A bartender-bot descends from the sky to hover next to him. "Blue vodka. Tall glass with four ice cubes."

The spherical robot repeats his order, then flies away.

"I was surprised to get your call," he says to her. "I wouldn't think such a distinguished family as yours would be interested in such a filthy business."

Another bartender-bot appears. This one has arm attachments and places a drink in front of him. Then it, too, flies away. Tai takes his initial sip from the tall glass.

"This business has made its way to my Spanish Americas. We feel that we must be more actively involved, so my associates and I are willing to pay our way to the head of the line," she says.

Tai smiles. "But of course. I would do no less in your position. If I can be of any assistance, I will help you, gladly."

"We understand that you have acquired the exclusive services of an American bio-scientist, a Doctor Mary."

"Your sources are quite impressive, not even my own government knows that."

"And they will never learn it from me or any of my associates. Discretion is fundamental to us in our business."

"But of course."

"We would be willing to pay you whatever rental fee we can agree upon to have access to her before you commence your business with her."

"Unfortunately, we are retaining her for an exclusive life contract. We will not be sharing her with anyone."

"No negotiation is possible?"

"We are both very wealthy people. At our level, money is less important than other considerations. We are heavily invested in bioengineering and all the genetic sciences for that matter, not the quaint bio-warfare aspects that concern governments. We are interested in the essence of life itself."

"You must forgive me because my people hear such rhetoric often, and all we get from such people are man-made life-forms of horrific construction—monsters.”

“Yes, I heard your country had a *scorpion* problem.”

“Yes, it did.”

“Those actions are of a childish, criminal class. We are interested only in higher ideals. We are interested in—forgive the religious reference—godhood. To be able to create life—whatever we can imagine.”

“Is that what you need Frankenstein Girl for?”

Tai laughs. “Yes, I heard that is her nickname. There is an international race for such scientists and my people are determined to win that game. Therefore, with great regret, I am unable to help you.”

“You are not working as a proxy for the CHINs?”

“No mademoiselle, we are not. My people are so beyond petty constructs of borders and nation-states. The world is one country and we will configure it any way we please.”

“The Internationalists?”

He smiles again. “Yes, a more preferable term to the other less respectful ones I’ve heard.”

“What will your group do with this ‘god’ power?”

“Mademoiselle, we are friends, but I cannot reveal such facts on even my most generous of days.”

“Clones and creatures. Killing and torture. Amusement of a new uber-rich elite—adult-children who have created their own pseudo-religion to justify their actions. In your world, there is no morality or immorality, no good and evil, only the strong and weak, the lucky and the victims, many victims.”

“Why does it matter, mademoiselle? The victims live in a world of self-amusement, too. Someone must occupy the top of the food chain.”

“Señor, it occurs to my associates and me that we can tolerate governments because they are doing their evil to protect their nations. Their behavior can be predicted and managed. But free agents are another matter."

"I compliment you, mademoiselle, as I am starting to understand your motives. Use an established member of one of the longest-standing, wealthiest families in the world to make contact with us. You ably exploited one of the key flaws of the uber-rich. We will always take a call from a fellow member. You've been used well."

"Señor Tai, I was used often in my Pagan youth, but as an adult born-again Believer, those days are a distant memory. I am used by no one in my new life, and both my old life and new life have vividly shown me that those who strive to be gods in this world never do it so to create paradise, only different variations of Hell on Earth."

"Mademoiselle, I feel the conversation has moved to possibly an unfortunate place."

"No Señor, it's the same place as always. The never-ending battle between good and evil."

He laughs. "But who is who, mademoiselle? It is easy to ask the question, but the answer is often not as black and white as some would want to believe."

"Hmm. I'm against creating creatures to attack and kill people so, forgive my presumptuousness, Señor, but I think that puts me in the army of goodness."

"For a beautiful woman who is visibly unarmed in her rather sleek, designer dress, it's too bad you didn't bring two weaponized cyborgs of your own to back up your threats."

"Señor, someone of my status never does that. I pay others to do that for me."

Tai has no time to react. The elevator entrance explodes and the two cyborg guards are blown apart. He jumps up from his chair and starts to turn his head back to her, reaching into his jacket for his weapon. All she does is point with her index finger. He is violently knocked back several feet into the glass wall by an invisible, concussion blast.

A drone shooter descends from the sky and riddles his chest with gunfire as he yells out.

Mona Lisa casually rises from her chair. Dozens of men come out of the stairwell door, some with weapons and others carrying body bags that are not empty. The body bags are quickly unzipped and the well-dressed dead bodies inside are taken out and posed on the ground; weapons placed in their hands. Others fire weapons all around, strafing the solid walls, shattering the glass walls, and destroying furniture and other objects. In moments, their work is done—the scene is staged.

"Make the call to the authorities," Mona Lisa directs one of her men.

Flight over the Pacific Ocean
12:02 a.m., 23 December 2095

Dr. Mary's face is shocked as she reads a message on her e-pad. She is the only passenger on the tiny stealth jet except for the one man who led her from her pod-car. Their seats are facing each other.

"What's wrong?" he asks, seeing her panicked expression.

She continues reading. "My buyer is dead. Some…gang shoot-out." She looks up. "I need to call my broker."

Secret Location, The Russian Bloc
8:26 a.m., 24 December 2095

The entire room is a giant sphere, with a myriad of messages scrolling continuously around its holo-wall. In the center of the room is an inclined desk with a stool attachment that seems to hover just above the ground. A retro phone hangs on one side of the desk and begins ringing. A hatch on the ceiling is thrown open, a ladder descends, and a man climbs down. He jumps to the floor and grabs the phone.

"Ya," he answers.

"Routing call," a computer voice says. "Client 2-3-5-9."

"Hold." The man puts the phone on pause as he sits on the stool at the desk. He puts on his clear glasses and the holo-interface activates. Externally the glasses seem to turn black, but from his vantage, he is surrounded by a floating computer vid-screen with many displays. All the information on Client 2359—Doctor Mary—displays with pictures, all transaction activity, payments, status, related news, etc. He puts the ear-set from his desk into his ear. "Yes, Client 2359."

"I have a major problem." He sees her voice wave on the display. The computer automatically analyzes all emotional factors and truthfulness indicators. Her agitation is genuine.

"Explain."

"My buyer is dead!" her voice yells. "What do I do now?"

He reads the newsfeed from his display. "Hong Kong police authorities found your buyer dead on the penthouse level of the HK Shangri-La Hotel. He and his bodyguards had a violent shoot-out with one of the city's anarchist gangs. That's the official story anyway."

"What do I do now?"

"Client 2359, I'm the matchmaker. I put one legitimate party in touch with another, that's it. I am not responsible for anything after that."

"I am in flight right now to Hong Kong, so what do I do? I need another buyer."

"Client 2359, if you are asking me to do another match, then I am happy to do that. But I can't do that instantly, and there will be another charge at the full price. I need time to work—"

"Didn't you hear me? I'm on the plane now, in the air to Hong Kong. I need a buyer now. And don't tell me you need time to work. You had a list of buyers, you said. Who was the next highest bidder?"

"Hold."

The list pops up on his display. He notices that four of the names on the list are showing as deceased or no longer interested, but he ignores the data.

"Client 2359, the next highest available bidder is a party in Australia."

"Available?"

"Yes. Lucky you, because everyone else on the list is unavailable."

"Just one buyer left?"

"Client 2359, that isn't unusual. Buyers come and go in this world. This is not a dating service. I'm matching you with fellow criminals."

"Were they the next highest bidder?"

"Lucky you. They were."

"Australians? Australians would have a higher bid than Russians or CHINs?"

"These Australians are Spanish."

"Okay. Send me the coordinates."

"Client 2359, are you forgetting something?"

"I'll transfer the money right away to the same account—"

"No, not to the same account! That account was closed. I will send the new account data to you."

"Okay."

"You'll have the coordinates as soon as the transfer is complete. Sent. Oh, thank you Client 2359."

Flight Over the Pacific Ocean
12:33 a.m., 23 December 2095

Dr. Mary looks up from her e-pad. "Tell the pilot we need to change course immediately."

"Sure." The man grins and gets up from his chair. "It's your money to burn."

Mary is sweating heavily and swallows hard as the man walks to the cockpit. With the click of a digital button, she is completely broke. A deal in Australia must happen.

Ibiza, Australia
2:42 p.m., 25 December 2095

Before it fell to the Supreme Islamic Caliphate in 2065, the original Ibiza was a tiny island of Spain in Western Europe. Its new Arabic name is unpronounceable to most, but the new tek-city of Ibiza in Australia was created by those Spaniards who were lucky enough to escape the violent end of their country and Western Europe.

Ibiza, Australia is home to primarily Spaniards, but also minority populations of Portuguese, Moroccans, and other ex-Western Europeans. If the Free Occupied Western Europe movement were ever to become real, between Australia and America, there would enough ex-pats to create an army. The tek-city is also a favorite destination stop for the wealthy from all over the world, especially the Spanish Americas (known as Latin America a half century ago)—from Mexico to South America. Just over three decades old, with the towering steel and glass buildings of the business district as its center, Ibiza is one of the country's main business centers, along with Sydney and Melbourne.

Ibiza is also the home of the Nuevo Museo del Prado—simply called Nuevo Prado. The original El Prado museum still exists in the city of Madrid in Islamic Spain, but the Caliphate is a closed territory to non-Muslims, and that museum is used as one of the residences of the country's Islamic Governor. At the Fall of Western Europe, a network of wealthy Spaniards was able to rescue most of its vast art as they fled the country, taking with them the collections of the Museo Thyssen-Bornemisza, the Museo Arqueológico, and the Museo Reina Sofía. Some museums survived the war, but others were destroyed in clashes between the Spanish population and invading Muslim armies.

Mona Lisa has always noticed that the New Australian Spaniards are very proud of the fact that they saved the most important pieces of Spanish art in the world; however, they never seem to be to upset about the tens of thousands of their countrymen, if not more, who were killed in the Fall. Maybe they are better at hiding their deep emotions than other expat Western Europeans. Maybe it's too painful to acknowledge.

Like every other tek-city in the world, hidden surveillance vid-cams are embedded in every physical structure, and surveillance drones hover in the skies. Nuevo Prado is no different. Mona Lisa has been watching Frankenstein Girl ever since she exited her taxi five miles away. Mona Lisa touches the shimmering white pearls around her neck—they never seem to go out of fashion. She is wearing a one-piece, golden, sleeveless dress with matching gold shoes. The woman she is watching from her desk vid-screen has the opposite of fashion sense—a thick brown coat over her gray-toned clothes and a black hat pulled low in an attempt to conceal her face (though tek-city surveillance can easily see through virtually all clothing materials).

Today is 25 December 2094—Christmas, of all days. Christmas for Catholics and the Eastern Orthodox. Ever since the Separatist Movement over two decades ago, Protestants celebrate the birth of Christ in March as part of their Christian High Holy days and interconnected with the High Holy days of Jews.

Nuevo Prado is one of the busiest attractions in Australia, with visitors worldwide. Mona Lisa watches the vid-feed of the woman entering the building. The woman is paranoid, more so than even a Faither, walking in circles, double-backing, and standing in place for minutes on end, obviously watching the people around her through the dark glasses on her face.

Almost an hour later, the intercom buzzes in her ear-set.

Mona Lisa touches the earlobe. "Yes."

"Señorita Gustavo, your appointment has arrived," a man's voice says.

"Please have her escorted up."

"Si, señorita."

Dr. Mary is led into the spacious executive offices by a large man in a white suit and tie. He gestures her in, then closes the door behind her. Mona Lisa sits quietly at her marble desk, her hands clasped together. The woman looks around the room with its magnificent art, antique bookshelves with real physical books, and a beautiful rug taking up almost the entire floor.

"Good afternoon, Señorita Mary." Mona Lisa is standing, ready to shake her hand.

Dr. Mary approaches her slowly. She seems uncomfortable with the idea of shaking hands. Mona Lisa nods instead and gestures her to sit in the chair in front of the desk.

"May I have some refreshments brought in?"

"No, thank you. I am fine for the moment."

"Do you wish to remove your hat and coat? You are permitted to do so."

The woman hesitates but takes off her hat, then her head scarf. Her brunette hair is tied back tight. She begins to take off her jacket.

"You can place your hat and scarf on the desk. It's okay."

"I'll just hold onto it."

"As you wish." Mona Lisa returns to her casual seated pose—legs crossed and hands resting on the desk, clasped.

Mary takes a moment to settle back in her chair. "You Spaniards have a beautiful country."

"Thank you, but I am Mexican."

"Oh."

"A simple mistake. Have you been in Australia long?"

"I arrived a few days ago."

"Nice flight?"

"I hate to fly, so it's never a nice thing for me. I can't wait until teleportation is invented. I would much prefer that."

"I would not prefer that ever, but you can use that method. It will leave more space on the plane for the less adventurous like me."

"I don't imagine space is ever a problem for you. You must have your own private jet at your disposal."

A smiling Mona Lisa asks, "Shall we transact our business, Señorita Mary? You also told my associates that you had some additional items that you wanted to trade for cash chips."

"Yes, untraceable cash."

Tek World is a cashless society—all money is digital. However, outside the main tek-cities—in the Outlands, Trog-land territories, and the criminal underworld—physical cash remains the safest allowable currency. It is a combination of anti-government paranoia and militant libertarianism, which gave birth to this off-Grid economy and the ability to do business (not necessarily criminal) outside the Grid's ever-watching surveillance. Anonymous cash chips of whatever desired denomination is what Mary wants.

"Not a problem," Mona Lisa says. "Nuevo Prado will give you fair market value for whatever items the museum can use. Since you do not have the items with you, may I ask for a brief description of the items and their provenance?"

"They are from private American collections. Do you know much about Jew-Christians?"

"Señorita, I come from Mexico. My home country has a significant religious population and a deep religious history, so yes, I am quite knowledgeable. I'm also an art collector where the intimate knowledge of all history, religious or otherwise, is required. What art do you have?"

"Art from Old Pre-Islamic Western Europe. The World War Two era. The original art would have belonged to Jew-Christians, but it's all historical at this point."

"Stolen art?"

"World War Two was a hundred and fifty years ago. The artwork is in immaculate condition. Priceless. I have all the authenticity papers."

Mona Lisa stares at her for a moment. "Are you saying you have stolen art from German Jews of World War Two by the Nazis?"

"Who owned it first doesn't matter, only the last owners. I have all the authenticity papers."

"And how do you have the art now?"

"I just do."

"How many items?"

"I believe seventy-six works."

"I see. Interesting. We can discuss the art afterward. Shall we get to the business at hand?"

Mary leans back in her chair. "Yes. I've decided to go with your last bid for my services. I'm ready to conclude today if you're ready to pay today."

"Tell me about the Keeper, Senorita Mary."

Mary's calm expression changes to surprise. "Who? I don't know who that is." She knows that her body language has indicated otherwise.

"Señorita Mary, please do not try to construct a series of lies to tell me. You are as bad at it as I am exceptional at spotting it. As of this moment, the only thing you may benefit from is a bag of cash chips for your Nazi-stolen art. The big payday you are expecting will never materialize unless you are honest and open with me."

"I am being honest. I don't know who that is."

Mona Lisa shakes her head. "There's a lie again. It looks like we won't be able to do business after all. We were so looking forward to having you on our team. Should I have my employee call you a taxi?"

"Your people told me that you needed the best bio-geneticist and engineer you could buy."

"You seem very comfortable in stating your new hobby to a person you just met. A hobby that would get you arrested, tried, and executed by your own American government."

Mary laughs to herself. "Governments have no right to restrict information from the people. The public should have open access to all genetic information, free access to genetic engineering and manipulation. We say we live in a democracy, but the Grid is one big government corporation run by an oligarchy that chooses everything for us. We should choose for ourselves."

Mona Lisa smiles. "Señorita, I thought you simply to be an

American traitor for hire, selling government secrets to the highest bidder. But you claim higher, noble ideals as your primary motivation. How is it called…the tek progressive movement?"

Mary smiles. "Yes, that's it."

"Pagans destroy the religious with one hand while creating their own with the other. Do the living organisms you create have any rights at all? Not to be modified according to your whims and perversities? Do you have an answer for me?"

Mary says nothing.

"Can I turn you into my personal creature? Maybe give you pink fur instead of skin, four legs instead of two, big bat wings from your back, or a long giraffe neck instead. Can I do that?"

Mary remains silent.

"Seems your tek progressive movement is nothing but excuses for sociopathic, narcissistic adult-children who feel they can do anything they want to another living thing. Just like the old labor slave trade of the past, the old fetus termination industry that used to exist prior to the bio-switch, and, my personal favorite, the sex-slavers of today. What was that scientist's name? Yes, Josef Mengele. He was a scientist too, like you. Señorita, my colleagues and I are not interested in your supposed ideological motivations or your political philosophy. Where is the Keeper?"

Mary speaks slowly. "I don't know anything about her, other than that she was a scientist. I assure you that whatever you want the Keeper for, I can do. She's dead or already captured by another government in a top-secret dungeon, never to be seen again."

"Why do they call you Frankenstein Girl?" Mona Lisa's tone is cold. She already knows the answer.

Mary hesitates. "I don't know. It's a stupid nickname. I was one of the leads on a genetic program to reanimate corpses and dead animals. The program was abandoned a long time ago for more productive projects. Why reanimate—"

"When you can create new organic organisms to quickly launch onto the battlefield," Mona Lisa interrupts.

"I don't know anything about the Keeper. I only met her once and that was a long time ago."

"Then we don't need you. You're only a marginally competent bio-scientist. We need what they call in your scientific circles, a 'god.'"

"Is that what you need? What about a goddess?" She tries to make a joke.

Mona Lisa taps her desk tablet. "I will try another approach. The dollar amounts that my colleagues discussed with you will be tripled if you can give us credible leads to this Keeper. We want her, not third-rate actors like you who do nothing but mimic her research."

"Why?"

"If we don't find her first, then someone else will."

"She's dead."

"She isn't."

"How do you know?" Mary asks, but Mona Lisa doesn't answer. "This isn't about creating biological units for you, is it?"

"No, it isn't. It's about acquiring all the people who can. You see, Señorita Mary, a few years ago one of the criminal cartels in my native country released scorpion-creatures into the general population. We are no longer talking about genetic warfare or even genetic terrorism, but genetic anarchy and biological chaos."

"Biological chaos?"

"My associates and I must intervene. The activities of your colleagues can now alter entire ecospheres, regionally and globally."

"That's ridiculous. I bet you're a Jew-Christian. When the atomic bomb was invented, they said the planet would go up in a nuclear apocalypse. Now most of the world is powered by fusion power. Science makes the world better. It always has."

"By creating things that should not exist in the planet's biosphere?"

"It's human progress. No one is altering the global ecosphere. That's just hysterical nonsense. Like global freezing, global warming, or artificial intelligence and robots taking over the world. You can't stop science, so what are you and your associates going to do?"

"Where is the Keeper?"

A thought pops into Mary's head. "You want the Keeper to kill her. Is that what this is about? This was all a ruse. You probably were responsible for my first buyer being killed, weren't you? I don't know where she is and since, according to you, I'm only a mediocre scientist, I'll be on my way. Yes, call me a taxi."

"You are very bad at this criminal thing, Señorita Mary, very bad. We've taken the liberty of letting Homeland Security in America know what you've been doing and they have responded by issuing a global arrest warrant for you. Scientific espionage is treason, even in America."

"You're bluffing and I'm not scared by anything you say."

"Living off the Grid isn't as easy as you would think."

Mary stands from her chair. "I'll sell my services to someone else."

"As you like, but I suspect your matchmaker will not be able to find any new buyers. I suspect he will not even accept your calls."

Mary stares at her, visibly trembling.

"You should never have ventured out of the laboratory, Señorita."

"You can just die." Mary violently shoves the chair away and starts for the door.

"I wouldn't do that if I were you, Señorita."

"Why?"

"American Homeland Security agents are waiting for you at all exits."

"They couldn't have located me this fast."

"True," Mona Lisa says. "But we called the local American Embassy the moment you walked through Nuevo Prado's front door. We reported that a crazy woman claiming to be an American scientist was causing quite a ruckus and scaring our visitors, yelling that she wanted to sell bio-warfare secrets to the CHINs—or did we say the Caliphate, or maybe the Russians? We told them she must be intoxicated but felt America should immediately take her in."

Mary stands there, not knowing what to do. "You're lying."

"Good day, Frankenstein Girl. It was a pleasure making your acquaintance."

"Are you going to let me leave here?"

"This is a public facility, Señorita Mary. You can leave whenever you wish. I don't care if you stay or go."

Mary walks slowly out of the room, but stops in the hallway. The man who led her into the executive office waits. He gestures for her to follow. She walks to him.

"She said that people are waiting for me at the exits."

"Yes, Señorita. The American Federal Police await you downstairs."

"If I give you money, will you tell me how to escape? You must have a secret exit somewhere."

The man laughs. "My boss pays me very well, Señorita, so I don't need any extra money. And there are no secret exits in Nuevo Prado. You must surrender yourself. That is the only way for you."

Mary runs back into the executive offices. Mona Lisa is looking at her vid-display, typing. "What do you want?"

Mona Lisa looks up from her desk. "I already told you, Señorita."

"I don't know where she is. We worked in different buildings, different shifts. I met her only once. Work teams don't mix. They kept us away from the superstars like her. I don't know anything about her. I told you."

Mona Lisa looks back down at her desk tablet. "I've seen what long-time prison incarceration can do to some people. They get to a point of the occasional suicidal thought, and then an insatiable impulse to destroy themselves takes over as time passes. It is the timid ones like you who are the first to break. I once heard of a prominent little politician woman in my country who is in federal prison for life. She slit her own throat to end her life because she couldn't take it anymore."

Mary looks up to the ceiling and closes her eyes. She opens them and there is a glint of tears. "Okay, I will do it. I'll help you. Don't let them capture me. Just get me away from the Homeland agents."

Mona Lisa stands. "Very good. I so hate torture. Persuasion is far better. Between you and Frankenstein Boy, we'll be able to piece together all the clues we need."

"Frankenstein Boy?"

"Yes, your colleague, Doctor Godwin, of course."

"He's in the District, Washington, DC. He's a deputy director for the Science Division."

"How did he get such a prestigious job? He's even more of a mediocre scientist than you are. Well, he is not as far away as America. He is here with us."

"Godwin is here, too?" Mary's eyes widen. "This was all a trap to get me from the start. You're going to kill us!"

Chapter Three: Niccolo

Ibiza, Australia
12 noon, 26 December 2095

Mona Lisa watches from the strip, wearing dark glasses and covered in a light coat, as a white hover-jet descends toward the private landing field. The aircraft's main wings start to recede into the body of the craft as the hover-engines engage; then the aircraft sets down with barely a sound. The main door opens and the auto-steps lower to the ground. Dressed in a full black suit, his shirt buttoned only halfway, Niccolo exits.

Mona Lisa smiles as he approaches and embraces her with a kiss on each cheek. To true friends he is known as Niccolo; to everyone else he is The Sicilian. He is in his late forties, has green eyes, and is naturally bald. Hair can be grown and every Pagan does so. It can even be corrected neo-naturally or with a pill. Faithers do neither. Who would have guessed that baldness would become one of the telltale signs of a religious person?

Niccolo is a senior leader in the New Catholic Order, like Mona Lisa. The world still did not know—one of the largest global secrets ever kept—that the Vatican in Rome had fallen to the Supreme Islamic Caliphate just five years ago. New Lerdo City in

Mexico is the New Vatican.

Mona Lisa turns and gestures to her men. They approach from the small airfield building, pushing two hover gurneys with a person strapped to each one. The men stop to allow Niccolo to examine the captives—one is Doctor Mary. Her eyes are red as she stares at him. A device is over her mouth and nose to regulate her breathing and a clear visor is over her eyes. A thick blue cable is attached to her chest above her heart, and her wrists, elbows, thighs, and ankles are securely fastened to the gurney. The other captive is a man who almost looks like her male twin—Doctor Godwin. He turns his head away and closes his eyes. Niccolo gestures to the men to continue on. They push the hover-gurneys to the plane's cargo hold.

"I officially turn the mission over to you," she says. "The Mexicans have done their part; now it's the Italians' show."

Niccolo laughs. "Yes, it is. Any loose ends remaining?"

"None, but be careful, though I know you always are. My sources in the Russian Bloc believe something is in motion there that could affect the mission." She sees his questioning look. "Witches and warlocks, I was told." She raises her hand as his face turns to disgust. "No need to say it. I know."

"I thought that's what is being loaded on the jet. Will you be returning to base?"

"A few more things to wrap up and then I will. The Protestants have traced this Delivery Man."

"Is your team going to take it?"

"We're going to maintain the trace and see where it leads."

"Then you be careful, too."

"We always are. God bless."

Niccolo smiles and gives her a final hug. "Wish I could stay longer and enjoy Ibiza, but the jungles are calling."

Over the Pacific Ocean
1:15 p.m., 26 December 2095

Godwin and Mary remain shackled to their seats in the center of the aircraft. They watch Niccolo, who is seated in a chair across from them, as he reads a physical book with a large red bookmark that he moves as he turns a page.

Godwin asks, "Is that what books used to look like? I can see why we got rid of them. Look how bulky, and that is just one of them. Like when a nano-computer today would take up every floor of a twenty-story building in the past."

"Kidnapping me is one thing, but he's a ranking member of the American government. You can't just snatch him." Mary's anger has been simmering for over an hour.

Niccolo ignores her.

"Why am I here?" Godwin asks.

"They want the Keeper," she says to him.

He looks at her with a surprised expression, then turns to Niccolo. "What do I know about her? She's dead. No one has seen her in five years. I don't know anything about her. Did I ever even meet her?"

"Once," Mary says to him. "Same time I did. That general meeting we had."

"That's right." He looks at Niccolo again. "There were hundreds of people in the room. We said two words to her."

Niccolo closes his book and leans forward. "I will spend no time trying to convince you or threatening you. We want the Keeper. I care about nothing else. You give me that information and you're free to go. That's the deal. Whether you accept or when you do is up to you. No one will ask, beg, or threaten. Incidentally, despite your consistent cover story, we do know she was your boss for ten years, but if you wish to continue pretending, then continue." He leans back and opens his book again.

Mary and Godwin are quiet for a moment. "Where are you taking us?" Mary asks.

Niccolo stands. "You'll know when we throw you out of the jet."

Godwin and Mary have been sitting for countless hours. There are no windows, and only an occasional bump from turbulence indicates that they are even in flight. Niccolo disappeared through a door to a forward compartment of the cockpit and never returned. Their shackles disengaged a while ago, and the rear aircraft lights switched on to show a single restroom door. But that is as far as their captors' hospitality has gone. The only things for them to do are sleep or stare off into space. Neither feels like talking, so they both try to sleep.

Mary is jolted awake by a rush of cold air. *She screams, realizing that she is falling through the sky! He was serious!* Her body is spinning and all she can see is Godwin falling too. In the opposite direction, the fast approaching green is everywhere—a vast jungle.

Parachutes open and their bodies are yanked up for a moment before they drift back down and into the dense jungle brush.

"We were drugged!" Godwin yells after ripping off his face mask.

Mary remains still with her eyes closed to calm her panic attack. She pulls off her own face mask and lets it fall from her hand. They must have put the masks on them in the middle of the night. They both dangle from the tree canopy about ten feet from the ground.

"We're still alive," she says softly.

"They want information from us so they'll keep us alive, but we have to escape somehow."

"We're lab rats. What do we know about escaping from

jungles? How do we even get down from here?"

"There's supposed to be a release latch somewhere on the chute."

"But we're too high."

"No, we're okay. Drop, don't lock your knees, and roll."

The two scientists find the release switches on the backs of their chutes. They fall through the branches and leaves of the tree to the ground without injury.

"We need to head to the water," Godwin says. "We can then try to figure out where we are from there."

Godwin is ready to go, but Mary remains seated on the ground.

"What's wrong?" he asks.

"They didn't drop us here for a vacation. And we're not going to be able to escape. This place is to make us talk. What do you think is here?"

"I don't know what's in their minds, but we can't stay here. Let's get to the water and figure out a plan from there."

Without any mobile or wearable devices, they can only guess at the passage of time. After hours of walking through the jungle, they both make the same observations. There is a clear dirt path along the level ground. The trees on either are of a wide variety of types, but very strange is the fact that there is not a sound anywhere—no animals and no birds. They don't even hear or see any insects.

Finally they reach the coast of the jungle and the canopy opens to a magnificent view of an immense body of water stretching into the distance as far as the eye can see. Godwin walks the remaining twenty feet of the dirt path into the water and cups a hand to taste it. "Salty," he says. "Ocean water."

"This jungle is obviously man-made, so the water could be unnatural, too," she says.

"An empty jungle just for us? Why? How do they think that will make us tell them something we don't even know to begin with?"

"We'll find out."

They sit near the water across from each other with a ring of stones between them. Neither knows how to make a fire and they know it will be dark soon. The air is getting chilly and they have to pull down the sleeves of their clothes to cover their hands.

"You would think as scientists we'd know how to make a simple fire." Godwin sighs. "They said Einstein couldn't do simple math. Maybe we are doing it right, but the sticks here are not capable of making fire."

"I've never seen fireflies before," Mary says, looking off into the jungle.

Godwin turns his head to look, too. He stares for a long time. After Mary turns her gaze to other things, he says, "Those are not fireflies."

Mary looks again. "What do you mean those aren't fireflies? What are they?"

"Fireflies fly. Those are not moving."

"Then what are they, glowing like that?"

"I think they are eyes."

Mary grabs one of the stones in front of them and begins to stand. "Animals? What animals have glowing eyes?"

"I don't know, but there are a lot of them." He stands and bends down to pick up a stone, too.

When she thought they were fireflies, she was pleased. Now that they might be animals, she notices that they are appearing in sets of two—they are eyes!

"Should we run into the water?" she asks.

"No, wait until they move to us."

The wind changes to a warm breeze. They can now hear birds and multiple animal noises in the distance, and sounds in the nearby water. The entire jungle has suddenly come alive!

"What's happening?" Mary says.

A roar rumbles in the distance, so loud that both of them jump.

"What was that?" Mary is so scared that she starts toward the water. "That sounded like a…what was that?"

Glowing eyes are moving to them from the jungle. If they are animals, there are hundreds of them. Both scientists run to the water. Mary looks around frantically to see if there is any other place to run. There is none. They stop at the water's edge, then slowly step back at the sight of movement underneath its surface— not one thing, but many.

Punjab Region, India (CHIN Territory)
9:43 a.m., 28 December 2095

All the cities in the region are retro tek-cities—historic architecture but outfitted with modern conveniences such as climate regulators to cool the hot air and auto-drive pod cars to patrol the streets, especially for the elderly to get about. No law enforcement or commercial drones are allowed here. People ride horses and camels in the streets and every religious temple is fitted with tek-jammers to keep some of the less religious followers from using mobile devices inside.

The limousine for Niccolo stops a few blocks away. The city is arranged in such a way that main streets allow vehicles to drive only on the outer perimeters encircling residential neighborhoods. Within these neighborhoods, the narrow streets are for walking only, though manual bicycles and Segways are plentiful.

Niccolo enjoys the casual walk as he follows a Sikh man, while another holds a day umbrella to shade him. Another follows behind them. After a couple of blocks, they arrive at what could only be called a small palace. It is a white building; a two-story religious temple with one-story residences.

"Sikh Bob, is it?" Niccolo extends his hand to the man waiting at the main door.

"Yes it is," he answers. "Non-Hindi speakers find my name too hard to pronounce, so a long time ago I found it easier to use a nickname."

"You have to write it down for me. I'll learn how to pronounce it."

Sikh Bob gestures for Niccolo to walk inside beside him. The other three Sikhs wait at the foot of the steps. Sikh Bob leads the Italian into the sitting room. The room is sparse with four chairs in a square formation around a rectangular floor carpet. The simple wooden center table has a bowl of fruit. There is a basic work desk filled with papers and physical books in one corner, and the entire adjacent wall is taken up by bookshelves with books that look as ancient as these lands. He gestures to Niccolo to sit at the corner of one of the couches while he seats himself on the adjacent one. There is a large open balcony with sheer white curtains fastened to either end of the wall. A nice, steady breeze blows.

"Moses and M say hello and so do Tova and Mr. Tova."

Sikh Bob smiles. "It has been a little while since we've had the pleasure of being in each other's company, but life as leaders of the Continuum must consume all their free time. Everyone outside of America still refers to it as the Resistance."

"We will always be the Resistance."

"Can I offer you some refreshments?"

"As long as it's something native."

Sikh Bob claps his hands and a woman appears from an inside entrance. He says something to her in Hindi and she disappears.

"You met the Moses and Tovas in Israel?"

"Yes." Sikh Bob nods his head. "Nearly forty years ago. We were all babies." He laughs a bit. "I didn't have a whisker of facial hair back then."

"Do you ever wonder to yourselves about how all of you met on that holy land tour in Israel? That maybe it was divine providence?"

"Like maybe the Founding Fathers of America?"

"Yes. One of the founding members of the African Collective converted to Catholicism after that trip. The chief general for the Mormons was also there."

"Yes, Vincent."

"The connections made there also led to the formation of the I-R-A, of all things."

"Yes, the bus driver's sister, Persia. I saw her last year. Yes, much came from that trip of strangers. Lifelong friends, lifelong alliances. Each one a leader."

"You have a fascinating background yourself. I am told that you are the only man in India who could become President by simply clapping his hands."

Sikh Bob laughs. "The power of my hand clapping goes no further than getting my last daughter to do an occasional errand until she gets married, too."

The young woman returns to the room with a tray of various food dishes, small cups, and a pitcher. Sikh Bob moves the fruit bowl to the corner of the table as she sets the tray on the table.

"Thank you daughter," he says.

She says something in Hindi to him and then to Niccolo says, "Enjoy."

"Thank you," Niccolo replies.

She disappears out the door again as Sikh Bob pours the drinks.

He gives Niccolo a variety of small plates of food. The only dish he recognizes is the curry rice.

"What is the politics like here in CHIN territory?"

"If you're Chinese or the Indian elite, it is wonderful. If you're the Hindi or Sikh masses, or even the Atheist masses, you have quite a different view. But the masses never organize; they only complain. The Alliance keeps the Muslims away, Kashmir and Jammu are firmly in Sikh hands, and the Hindus have their holy lands, so everyone accepts the status quo."

"So why aren't you President of India?" Niccolo finishes off another small plate. "Delicious."

"My mother told me that I was born to be a wartime president. Now that I am an adult, I know that to be true. I am ill-suited for leading in peacetime. Besides, the presidency in India is merely a figurehead post for the elite. Beijing is the real power."

"What does a warrior do in peacetime?"

"He visits his children, plays with his grandchildren and great-grandchildren, and tries to be a good religious role model in his retirement." He smiles as he sips from his cup.

The men finish their food and drinks. Sikh Bob pours them water from another pitcher.

"How do your people like Mexico?" Sikh Bob asks.

Niccolo leans back in the couch with his cup. "We have accepted that we will never return to the land that used to be our beloved Italy. But we have created New Italy, a new home."

"Neo-Italy," Sikh Bob corrects with a grin. "We're almost in the twenty-second century. Everything is 'neo' with the youth today. They think anything that existed before them is old. You have a Neo-Vatican, too."

"Yes, we do."

"For a very long time the Sikh had no homeland. Now we do

and I wish we didn't. The Sikh Order has become as corrupt, decrepit, and lazy as the Indian government. It is the real reason I am not publicly involved in politics anymore. I can't bear it. You walked here. Didn't you see all the men with pink turbans, yellow polka-dot turbans, neon-whatever color turbans, holo-turbans? Sacrilege."

"At least you have a homeland."

"We do, but in a few generations it will continue to be filled with men who wear turbans and not one of them will be Sikh. But you didn't come all this way to hear me lament."

"I relate completely. The struggle of faith is one that we all are very familiar with."

"How can I help my friends in the Continuum, Mr. Niccolo?"

"How interconnected is the Indian government with the Chinese government?"

"Not connected at all. The Chinese tells us only what they want us to do and the Indian government is happy with the arrangement. Information? The Chinese tell us nothing."

"True, but I'm sure more *assertive* elements within your country would aggressively gather intelligence on enemies and allies alike, including the Chinese."

"Yes, they would."

"They might be particularly interested in various war-games being conducted in CHIN territories."

"Yes, they might."

"If it's in CHIN territories, being conducted by CHIN authorities, then India should know as well. After all, there is no CHIN without India."

"True, but you must know I am not officially part of the Indian government anymore."

"But you have many friends."

"Only among the traditionalists, and they are an ever-shrinking minority in the government."

"But they are still part of the government and still have access."

"What is it that you need to know, Mr. Niccolo?"

"We need your direct help. You remember the Hat Yai experiment in '75?"

Sikh Bob nods as his expression changes from amiable to angry. "Yes, elements within the Thailand government's great, grand experiment for 'scientific' reasons. Erase all morality in a population; erase any concept of good and evil that was inherent in the people. It was all directed by outside foreigners. Changing the population's opposition to forced child prostitution to complete acceptance and advocacy. Outrageous and disgusting. When we found out, the Sikh Order along with the Hindus and the leadership of the Asian Consortium, we all swore that we would never allow such a thing to ever happen in our region again. We'd kill anyone who ever tried it again."

"And rightly so."

Sikh Bob grabs a couple of tangerines from the table bowl. "The Thailand experiment was a terrible scandal in the '80s when it was revealed to the public. It toppled the entire government." Sikh Bob pauses for a moment to look at his guest. "Please tell me that you're not about to tell me it is happening again."

"Various rogue forces are using uninhabited islands within the region for numerous experiments that we believe neither the Asian Consortium nor India Proper are aware of. We believe these experiments must be stopped and everyone involved must be neutralized."

"What are they doing?"

"Making monsters."

Sikh Bob's eyebrows rise even though he's looking at the food.

"The rumors of the scorpion-creatures in Mexico were true then?" he asks.

"Yes, but we're talking about a scenario far more catastrophic. The scorpion creatures we eradicated were not capable of reproducing. We believe that these new monsters can. And due to the location of these islands, if subjects from the islands were to escape—"

"You want me to notify the leadership of the Indian government? Have the islands searched and the experiments destroyed?"

"Such facilities could not be built without the direct authorization of the CHIN government or from elements within the highest levels." Niccolo lowers his voice. "You must proceed assuming that the Indian government *does* know about the islands."

"Most of them are bastards, but none of them would be so low."

"Are you sure?"

Sikh Bob looks at him for a moment. "There is nothing for someone to bribe them with. They have all the money they could ever spend; all their vices are amply satisfied. Most importantly, they would be afraid of the scandal if the people were to find out. What could they be bribed with?"

"That's what we must find out, but again I caution you, we don't think it's the Pagans alone in the Indian government hierarchy."

Sikh turns his gaze out the window. He looks back at Niccolo. "I hope your suspicions are wrong."

"We always hope that the scenario we fear the most is not true."

"What will you do while I make my private inquiries?"

"We'll prepare until you gather your facts."

"What if it is the CHIN government?"

"Then we won't strike."

Sikh Bob seems surprised by his answer.

Niccolo continues, "If it is the governments—CHIN, America, Russian Bloc, Spanish Americas—we can manage that. If it is as we suspect, independent rogue elements, then we can't allow that."

"Interesting position for the Continuum to come to, but I agree. I will find out what you need to know, but what precipitated this? Did something happen?"

"Yes." Niccolo pauses as he drinks from his cup. "I'll have one of the specimens delivered to you. Sometimes words are wholly inadequate for some situations."

Private Airport, Punjab Region, India (CHIN Territory) 8:20 a.m., 29 December 2095

Sikh Bob stares at it. Five other Sikh men, among them a medical doctor, are with him, their mouths hanging open. The creature lies on the cargo floor while the tarp that was covering it is pulled back more by one of Niccolo's men.

"How many of these *things* are out there?" Sikh Bob asks.

"In the open seas…there's no way to know," Niccolo answers.

Sikh Bob shakes his head. "I am formally requesting a meeting with the Continuum. It's been some time since I studied biology and ecology, but if this isn't contained, we could wake up one morning and find the planet crawling with life, evil life, that should never have existed. Please tell me you know the scientists involved with this abomination."

"We have some of them and we plan to deal with many, many more."

"This is an affront against God," the Sikh doctor says. "Why are they doing this?"

"Because they can," Niccolo answers.

"What else are they doing?" the doctor asks. "Is our government doing these things, too?"

Sikh Bob answers, "Of course they are."

Another Sikh man says, "We have been so worried about AI-controlled bombs, space-to-ground killer satellites, killer robots…but man-made monsters."

"If another world war ever does come, not one bird, fish, plant, insect, or human being will want to be anywhere near this miserable planet," Sikh Bob says.

He gestures to his man to cover the creature back up with the tarp—a greenish twelve-foot-tall shark-like creature with rows of giant razor teeth, two arms with clawed hands, and octopus tentacles for its tail.

Chapter Four: The African Collective

Theodore Hertzl Jewish Enclave, North Carolina (Five Years Ago)
9:16 a.m., 15 May 2090

The Jewish enclave is more metropolitan than most Faither cities—definitely not Orthodox or Hasidic, who prefer simple, plain, rustic communities. This is the joint community of the Mizrahi, the Arab and Persian Jewish Orders.

Everyone is preparing for the meeting and the security is formidable. The paramilitary Jewish 'Wolf Pack,' mostly men with shaved heads, dressed in black and heavily armed, as well as burly Persian and Arab Jewish security men. The two men—the key speakers—are led to the general conference hall.

Standing in front of the crowd, Gideon continues his presentation to the Jewish Continuum members. Well-dressed in a dark suit, he is clean shaven, with blond hair and gray eyes. Gideon is the real deal. Homeland Defense and Intelligence Agency, United States of America, Florida field office was his career until recent days. However, he is not here in his official capacity, but as an agent of all Jewish Orders. "You have the full overview of the facts."

Rabbi Oren yells, "Why would they do such a thing? What's your theory, Mr. Gideon? You worked in the government. Law enforcement, security, intel."

Gideon thinks for a moment. "Biologics warfare. Clone armies, super-soldiers, creating new life for military purposes."

"I thought all military spending was tek-related. Robotic armies, better drones, better attack vehicles for air, land, sea, and space," Rabbi Kanter says.

"They're doing both."

New Judea, South Sudan Land, Africa
6:42 a.m., 30 December 2095

Niccolo gazes out the window at the ground below as the jet begins its descent. The city may not be as massive as other tek-cities around the world, but those cities are not technically in a hot-zone, not unlike what used to exist for Jewish Israel before its fall to the Islamic Caliphate in 2081. The Muslims thought they would be able to take Africa as easily as they had done with all of Western Europe in 2065. Initially they were winning the war in Africa, but by 2088 they had been decisively stopped by the African Collective—a coalition of Protestant Christians, Coptic Christians, Armenians, Ethiopian Jews, various deists, and agnostics, led by Catholics. The Christo-Islamic War (or Islamic-Christian War) was over. Today a permanent stalemate remained at the Fifteenth Parallel, with the Christian South controlling three-fourths of the continent and the Caliphate holding onto the Northern part of Africa.

The jet touches down on the private runway. He can already see a five-man delegation of native Africans waiting. In this part of the world, the dress is much more diverse than anywhere else in the world—western suits, Arabic dress, long hooded cloaks, gym suits, casual clothes, lots of kufi hats, and lots of baseball caps. Two of the men are in simple t-shirts and jeans, while another wears sheer casual pants and a casual jacket with no top underneath. The other wears Arabic dress with a cross dangling from the necklace around his neck (an Arab Christian), and the fifth man is dressed all in black with a brown fez. All are wearing high-tek clear glasses. Niccolo imagines his very soul is being scanned every which way as he walks from the jet to greet them with firm handshakes.

The desert SUV rolls out of the airport parking lot and turns onto the busy road after two motor-cyclists whip by.

"Archbishop Masai is looking forward to meeting with you again, Mr. Niccolo," the man with the brown fez says as he turns in the passenger seat to look at him.

Niccolo sits behind the driver. The other men are sitting in the rear seats, facing out to watch the rear.

"I am, too. It has been over a year, much too long. We are all too busy with life. We must make more time for friends."

"Yes, Mr. Niccolo, very true. Was your flight from Asia nice?"

"Yes, it was. Thank you. Is there anything new on the border? There seemed to be more forces there when we flew over it."

"The Muslims don't cause trouble anymore."

"They are much too scared of their own people nowadays," the driver says. "Muslims try to come across the border every day to escape the Caliphate. They convert to Christianity, Judaism, anything to escape and stay here."

"Mr. Niccolo, are Bibles and Torahs illegal in the Spanish Americas like they are in Caliphate, America, and CHIN territories?" the man with the fez asks.

"Some Mexican countries still have them as illegal, but none of those laws are enforced. Most religious people live outside the tek-cities so the government doesn't bother."

"In the '80s, we had Muslims wanting to come to Christian Africa not to join the war on our side, but to be able to just live within our territory with their own Korans. Korans in any language that is not Arabic are illegal in the Caliphate and punishable by imprisonment or death." He laughs. "Do you know what Archbishop Masai did during the War? He had us drop leaflets along the border that said: *'Christian Africa lets you read your holy books in your native language from God and not the language forced upon you.'* It was so effective, the Caliphate moved all their forces back fifty miles and desertions and defections increased."

"Have you heard of the I-R-A?" Niccolo asks.

"Yes, we know of them. They are different here than in America," the man in the fez says. "Here they are mostly 'coyotes,' helping Muslims escape Caliphate lands. In America, they are the activists and only do politics. Nobody here cares about politics."

"God, family, food, shelter, and survival," the driver says. "Those are the politics of Africa."

"Very simple," Niccolo says.

"Yes, Mr. Niccolo, we prefer simple."

He nods. "I see little automation and mechanization in Africa."

The driver glances at his rear-view mirror. "Robots, you mean, Mr. Niccolo?"

"No, not necessarily. Tek in general."

"We have all the tek we need," the driver says. "And we passed laws years ago to ban cyborgs unless medically necessary. That's why you won't ever see the Japanese here."

Japan has the highest percentage of elective cyborgs in the world.

"We do have robots and drones, too," the man with the fez says. "But if you ever see one of them, it means you've been doing bad and they're about to kill you."

Science Division Building, Elizabeth Center, Anacostia, Southeast Washington, DC
9:23 a.m., 19 December 2095

Garrison stands in the hall with one of his men. They wait for a few passersby to enter the elevators before speaking again.

"Sir, now we have two scientists missing from our Zoo Project," the aide says.

"Who?"

"Doctor Godwin is the latest one."

Garrison is unconcerned. "It's fine."

"Sir?"

"We only gave him the position to see how secure the facility is. Obviously, the facility is not secure at all, and the division is unable to keep the identities and whereabouts of its personnel secret even though it's supposed to be an ultra-secret black site. It's what we needed to know."

"So…we do nothing, sir?"

Garrison smiles. "I have a meeting to go to, but have everyone waiting for me when I return. The President has a new interim directive for us. I'll explain then."

"Yes, sir."

10:03 a.m.

Four men sit in the tiny conference room watching a movie reenactment as it ends on the vid-screen.

"Lights," Garrison says and the overhead lights turn on, though the room remains dimly lit.

He stands and drags his chair around the table so that he can sit and face the other three men. Retired General "Tiny" Garrison is a small man, but he is the President's handpicked Division Director of the White House's ultra-secret Project New People.

"Here we are again. Has everyone reviewed the files?"

The other men nod.

"If I could ask, sir…"

"Yes?"

"The reports clearly identify leaks and outright espionage within the Science Division, which would logically suggest or demand apprehension or neutralization operations, but the conclusion, if I'm reading you correctly, is non-action. That can't be correct."

"When I started my career as a young man, I learned that there are always those segments of the general population that believe themselves to be smarter than the state. They think they know better when they actually know nothing at all. We have crossed the threshold. Our sister division in the Project will soon be able to create robotic life unlike we ever thought possible. But it is our division that has hacked the elements of life itself. We may be cheating to create new life now, but the creation of new life without any original organic material is within reach. Those are the stakes, gentlemen, but we have actors with their own infantile agendas who threaten that."

"But, sir, we know who the traitors are. Some are doing it for money, some for ideology. We must task resources to neutralize them."

"Why do that when others can do so for us?"

His men look at him, puzzled.

"Am I correct that there are Jew-Christian do-gooders who view our work as abominations against their gods?"

"Sir, you can't seriously mean to—"

"Am I correct that they believe that eliminating those involved in this work to be holy work of some type?"

"These are designated terrorists, sir," says one agent.

"Work with terrorists, sir?" asks another. "Will that be our directive?"

"All these activities are based outside our tek-cities, outside America even. All these criminal and espionage activities are based there. Should we send our own resources into outer-tek city regions? Why? Let these Jew-Christian true-believers do our work."

"How do we do that, sir?"

"They are already doing that work for us."

"What does that mean, sir?" another man asks.

Garrison touches his tablet and an image flashes on the wall—a whale-like creature with multiple tentacles for its tail. "This fine specimen was found in the Pacific Ocean. Gentlemen, they're in the ecosystem. It's one thing for us to conduct bio-operations in carefully controlled and monitored environments. It's even acceptable and expected if our enemies do so. We all clean up our messes. But rogue actors, with no loyalty to any nation or humankind at all, without any limits or safeguards…I have been directed to ensure that all these actors are…terminated."

"We're going to work with terrorists to accomplish this, sir?"

"We worked with Communists against the Nazis during World War Two. We worked with Nazis after World War Two against the Communists. We worked with Communists against Muslim terrorist countries. We worked with Muslim terrorist countries against Muslim terrorists. Alliances change all the time. The primary fear is this becoming a potential biological time-bomb for us and everyone else on the *planet*."

"What about the CHINs, the Caliphate, and the Russian Bloc, sir?"

"The President has been in the planning stages with the Russian Bloc President for the first-ever international summit of the world's current superpowers, to be held in Moscow. He broached this subject with all his global counterparts, all attending this summit, and they were all in agreement. We had the Frankenstein Project to attempt to reanimate fallen soldiers on the battlefield to be able to fight or at the very least shield their fellow soldiers. It was not to be used to replicate the Frankenstein movies of the past or to create a neighborhood zombie. The Robo-Man Project was to attempt to create the most advanced battle-ready cyborgs ever made, but reversible. It was not supposed to be for criminals to mechanize themselves for criminal activity or for people to give themselves mechanical genitalia. Legitimate bio- and robo-tek being turned into the frivolous, criminal, and disturbing. Frivolous and criminal is one matter, but disturbing is another. I'm not talking Jew-Christian moralities. The disturbing aspect of all this is the danger to national security and the Homeland.

"We've been instructed to clean this up before we get to the point of no return for not just America but all the superpowers. All *independents* must be neutralized—all of them, no matter their home country. We are now working for the USA *and* the world."

One of the man leans back in his chair. "And we'll allow Jew-Christian terrorists to neutralize them for us?"

"We'll even encourage it."

"Sir, my uncle was at the Kansas Event. He barely survived. The Jew-Christians are not Trogs and they're not stupid. We aren't using them, they're using us."

"We're all using each other and the one who can kill the other first, determines who was the smartest. For now, there can be no unsanctioned 'menageries' outside any of the governments of the world superpowers."

"I can't believe the CHINs and Caliphate agreed to allow America to take point on this, sir."

"I'm not surprised. In their minds, they get us to do their dirty work for them, too. The goal, gentlemen, short- and long-term is to protect the Homeland and our nation's interests. Science is war, too, and scientists are its soldiers. But if the President and the world want us to use religious terrorists to win this battle, so be it."

New Judea, South Sudan Land, Africa
7:32 a.m., 30 December 2095

There was another reason that people coalesced behind the Christians in Southern Africa when the Christo-Islamic War began. They ran the region better. Corruption in Africa was not confined to any one people or religion, but somehow the right people emerged when they were needed. Here, it was Archbishop Masai of the African Catholic Order.

As they drive through the streets, Niccolo cannot help but notice how much things have changed from when he was in the region decades ago as a young man. Then it was chaotic, with animals everywhere—chickens, goats, bulls, etc. The streets were filled with franken-cars—patched together with parts from all types of vehicles, old and new. What he sees today is a real modern tek-city.

The city is more advanced than his old town in Sicily before its fall to the Caliphate. The roads are filled with modern vehicles in auto-drive, with the notable exception of taxis zipping through traffic. The sidewalks and bridges over the streets are bustling with people. Most of the people are in casual dress, both modern and traditional, but there are those in suits even in this heat. Despite its tek, this is primarily an agricultural region and there are still the chickens, goats, cows, bulls, and sheep. The only things missing are the monkeys and elephants as he saw in India.

The New Judea Catholic Church is an exquisite, towering,

white castle-like building. Externally it has a simple construction, but inside he sees the most advanced tek-integration, much like the new Vatican in Mexico, multi-level, but open and airy with the same all-white theme. The ground floor has outer holo-walls streaming and rotating images of the breathtaking sites of the African continent. The inner walls are all transparent glass and there is much activity in progress. This church is the center of the city.

They enter one of the elevators and it rises. There are no indicators on the wall to show how many floors up they ascend. The doors open and there waits a contingent of Catholic Masai warriors—three men, extremely tall (the shortest being no less than six feet five) and dressed in black western suits.

"Good morning, Mr. Niccolo," the lead guard says.

"Good morning," he answers amiably.

In Old Italy, the Catholic Christians had the Swiss Guard as their special security force to protect the Vatican. For the New Catholic Order and the New Vatican, it is the White Guardsmen, the Texas Catholic enclaves that relocated to Mexico to take on the role. Every member group of the Continuum has its own advanced internal security service to protect its leaders. In Africa, the Catholic Masai, the indigenous warrior people that converted to Catholicism are the protectors of Africa's Vatican and its leader.

The guards lead the way while the two men who escorted him to this point remain in the elevator.

Niccolo glances down and realizes that they are, in fact, "walking on water"—a thin layer separates his feet from the crystal blue water. He sees there are things swimming below.

"Crocodiles," the lead guard says.

Niccolo looks up at him with a smile.

"I knew you would ask."

"I'm going to tell Father Marcos about this," Niccolo says, still amused.

"I'm sure for Mexicans and Italians, you'll have sharks."

"Great idea," Niccolo says, half-laughing.

"In Africa, those man-eaters don't mean much because they aren't indigenous," the Masai warrior adds.

The ground becomes solid white tiles and the Catholic Masai guards lead Niccolo to the Archbishop's residential offices, where they are greeted by an African Catholic nun.

"Mr. Niccolo," she says. "We are happy to meet you."

"Thank you."

"The rules."

"Rules?" A quizzical look on his face.

"This is a House of God. No cursing, no smoking, and keep your feet off my furniture."

Niccolo starts to laugh. Catholic nuns are the same everywhere.

He is taken to a large office with little furniture for its size. In the center, three small couches are arranged around an oval table. Only the driver and the man with the fez are with him now. The nun returns with a tray of beverages and sets it on the table.

Archbishop Masai enters the room. He does not say a word as he walks toward Niccolo to exchange a firm hug with a pat on the back. "God has blessed you with a safe and speedy trip to us, my friend."

"Archbishop, so happy to see you again."

"How is our mutual friend?"

"Father Marcos gets busier every day as we get closer to the inauguration."

"Please, let's sit."

Niccolo shakes hands with the two men as they leave the room.

"I will see you on your way out, Mr. Niccolo," the nun says as she leaves, closing the door behind her.

The men know each other well. Archbishop Masai's life is a remarkable one. His nickname is the "Cat," as it is said that he has nine lives, having survived unscathed multiple assassination attempts, accidents (his limo drove off a cliff in the rain and flipped seven times), natural disasters (the greatest sandstorm in known African history), a stampede of elephants, a cougar attack, and a plane crash. "Sounds like the plot of an amazing movie," he often says. "Except it's all true. I was the one who almost died each time, I wasn't laughing, and there wasn't a stunt double in my place."

The Archbishop is also the second-highest-ranking Catholic in the world. He is not just the leader of the African Collective, but also its supreme general of war operations, a position he has held since the Christo-Islamic War began fifteen years ago.

"How are things progressing?" he asks.

"Our guests seem to be ready to give us the information we need," Niccolo answers.

"What is the term they have for these things?"

"MMLs. Man-made life-forms."

"Even the Pagans realize the Pandora's box they have opened, and all the little ones too. Are you convinced you can find this Keeper?"

"I'm convinced that we can compile enough information for the Magi to find her."

"We're coming to the end and there is still so much to be done. For the first time in my life, I have seen more than just two Magi."

Niccolo is surprised. "Why?"

"The demons are back."

"Demons? There's more than one?"

"Oh yes, that's what has been occupying their Order. The

information your people gather from these bio-scientists is critical. There are too many rogue actors at play. Different regions, different areas of operations, different sources of financing, differing politics and objectives, but we need to identify all of them."

"We have our best *mind-benders* verifying their information. Are your sources convinced the Zoo exists?"

The Archbishop nods. "It exists."

Chapter Five: The Magi

Monster Island, Indian Ocean
10:44 a.m., 2 February 2096

Mary stares back. Her face is dirty, her hair disheveled, and she barely fills out her red jumpsuit uniform from all the weight she has lost.

"How did you even get control of this island?" she asks. "These places are always under the protection of a local government."

"You are right," Niccolo answers. "But protection is easily withdrawn if the right money exchanges hands. They protect us now and allow us to do whatever we want."

"I told your people everything," she says. "Every mundane, meaningless detail you wanted to know. I told them everything."

Niccolo smiles from his chair, facing her. "Have you?"

"I told them everything."

"I'm sorry about your friend."

Mary's face flashes anger. "No you're not. Are you going to throw me to those monsters to be eaten, too? Is that your plan?"

"I plan to do exactly what I told you on the plane when you first arrived here. There is only one proviso."

"I knew it," Mary says, shaking her head.

"You will be allowed to leave when the island is clear."

"Clear?"

"When it is clear of every last unholy, unnatural animal on the island, you can leave."

"I had nothing to do with this island."

Niccolo picks up his foldable tablet from his lap and opens it. "Do I need to recite all the places you did work, list all the 'animals' you made that others had to clean up for you? Others cleaned up your mess and now you will clean up theirs."

Mary's eyes are tearing up as she laughs. "Impossible. To completely clear an ecosystem like this would require far more than killing an animal here or picking up another there. It requires complete level-one quarantine of the entire area, armies of people, scanning, all surrounding areas must be…I don't even know all the procedures."

"We estimate that it will take you about a decade or so to restore the ecosystem to its natural state. We have assembled all the personnel and resources you need. We have even relocated your family to keep you company while you work."

Mary cocks her head back with a surprised look. "Family? I have no family."

Niccolo stands from his chair. "Your daughter is already en route. I will have someone show you the facilities that will be your new home and the base of your operations."

Mary slides off the chair and kneels on the floor before him, with her hands clasped together. "Please, don't bring her here. She can't see me like this, here. I'll do whatever you want, just don't bring her here."

"It's already done. She will be here today."

"Why are you doing this to me?"

"Why did you do this to others?"

"I was a government employee doing my job."

"You are an evil person on the market willing to sell her services to spread these biological atrocities across the planet. Have you forgotten so fast how we acquired you and your friend?"

"He wasn't my friend."

"And you don't have any family either? I hope the information we received from you is in fact the truth since you have so much trouble speaking the truth in normal conversation."

"Everything I told your people is the truth."

"We'll see."

"I don't want my daughter here."

"Why? Too bad she missed seeing her father alive, but where else should she be if not with her parents—Frankenstein Girl and Frankenstein Boy. You'll be sufficiently motivated in your new life's work."

Mary glares at him.

"You can give me all the dirty looks you want. If it were up to me I would have thrown you out of the plane without a parachute the day I saw you. I've seen your creations. I've seen the data about the sim-clones you made. What were you all planning to do with your Hitler, Stalin, and Mao sim-clones? Watch millions die for your personal amusement, your scientific studies? Get up from the floor!"

Mary slowly does.

"For a sub-species that doesn't believe in God and hates anyone who does, you all spend a lot of time trying to be your perverted version of Him, you evil woman. You will do as I say, without complaint, or I'll throw you to the same thing that ripped your friend-lover to pieces. It's okay for you to destroy innocents, but *you* must be protected from harm. Don't even look at me now!"

Monster Island (18 months ago)
1:02 p.m.

The Surveillance Room is only one level, but seems to go on forever. The top two-thirds of the walls are vid-screen displays of the entire island. Surveillance guards with black caps and black uniforms sit in front of specific display stations, spaced six feet apart. The guards never take their gaze from the display. They are always watching. The guards look physically identical in every way.

Mr. Oliver leads a group of men through the hall. In his shiny black suit, he is dressed as immaculately as they all are. The other men are in grays, blacks, navies, tans, and whites.

"As you can see, the facility has better security than even the White House in America or the Presidential Palace in Beijing," he brags.

"Why do you say that?" one man asks.

"Our system is completely automated—android guards for internal security, battle robots for perimeter security, sonic defense walls, anti-electro-magnetic defense walls, full weapon systems. All controlled by the most advanced AI computer brain."

"No human presence?"

"None. I've never understood this biological bigotry against mechanization. Biological beings are superior for strategy and creativity. For everything else, machines are far, far superior. On our island here they even regulate, maintain, and repair themselves, better than any human could."

He leads the men around the corner to the Surveillance Room. The men see for themselves the android guards at their seated posts.

"The other benefit of mechanization is that they never stop working." Oliver grins and says, "And we never need to pay them."

"Power source?"

"Fusion, of course. Independent to the island. Well-hidden and well-secured. We take the security of our creations very seriously."

"Any legal vulnerabilities?" asks one of the men.

"None at all. All of this is internationally legal. Thanks to animal rights activists, there are laws against using animals for military operations, but that applies to natural animals. We don't deal in natural animals. We grow our advanced, genetically modified, hybrid creatures for all your military needs in any climate, any environment, any place in the world. Doing business means the ability to protect your interests from any individual, group, or nation-state with the best in man-made life-form bio-weaponry."

"Do the androids manage the MMLs, too?"

"They do. The only humans are at separate lab facilities where new ones are created."

"So there should be no humans walking around in any part of the island?"

Oliver stops for a moment to glance back at the man with a questioning look. "That is correct. Why?"

"Then who are they?"

The man points. Everyone looks at the vid-screen display on the wall. Two people are walking through the jungle terrain of the island—a man with dark tan skin, and short, curly black hair. He is dressed in a white suit with white slip-on shoes. A woman walks next to him. She has a fair complexion, and blond hair tied in a ponytail. She wears a black suit, black heeled boots, and a black top hat on her head.

"What!" Oliver yells. "The alarms are not sounding."

He grabs the first seated android and it falls to the ground. The robot's eyes are flashing red. Oliver freezes with a shocked look. "That can't be."

"What's happening?" one of the men asks.

"It's in reboot mode."

Oliver lurches forward to manually activate the facility alarms by pressing a virtual button on the vid-screen. "Gentlemen, to the elevators! We will get to the secure level—"

All they hear is an explosion of animal sounds coming from outside the surveillance room. There are roars, howls, hyena laughs, and other noises. Along with the commotion, the sounds are getting louder and closer.

"Run!" Oliver yells. "The facility has been breached!"

The men run as fast as they can, but most can't help but look back. The 'animals' pour through the main doors. The pack of giant baboon creatures with clawed, reptilian forearms and rhinoceros-armored bodies—each of the animals alternates between lion roars, hyena laughs, and monkey screeches—jumps after the men.

Oliver reaches the elevators first as he frantically tries to make a call with his phone pen. "Priority red! Facility breached!" He keeps repeating his words, not seeing a baboon creature sneaking up behind him. Its mouth widens enormously and it pounces forward, biting off the upper half of Oliver's body.

The screams and carnage can be heard from every corner of the facility. The ceiling glows red and turns to sand, crumbling to the ground below. The two people the men had seen on the vid-display are the Magi—Wings and Top Hat. They descend through the new opening, as if by magic, to land quietly on the floor. With them are dozens of silver skeleton robot troops that also fly down through the opening to stand around them.

The skeleton robots use pulse blasts to move the baboon creatures back outside the building. The creatures run away and leap onto the trees, disappearing from view, but their wild animal sounds continue.

The two Magi step over the remains of the human visitors. Top Hat touches one of the vid-screen displays and Niccolo's face appears on every screen.

"The Magi Order formally turns over the facility to the New Catholic Order."

"We're on our way."

Little Rock, Arkansas
5:41 a.m., 6 February 2096

When people say "the Grid," they can mean any number of things. It is the tek-city's infrastructure, its automated control systems, the networked air-regulator machines constructed into almost every building to cool and warm the outside air, the fusion energy network to power every machine, large and small, directly and wirelessly; it is the auto-drive transportation system; it is the government's security and intelligence network of stationary (Eyes) and aerial vid-surveillance (drones); it is the synonym for the government itself. There are even secret Grid sub-offices near every Governors' primary office in all fifty-three states.

The town streets are quiet and only an occasional vehicle drives by. There is an orange glow visible from the second floor of a nondescript, three-story building near the main expressway—a secret government satellite office for the Grid. Moments later, the whole floor bursts into flames.

A half hour later, the street is still on lock-down as the robotic fire crew prepares to depart. One of the fire-bots continues to document by filming with its head-cam the now-blackened second floor of the building. Government officials arrive and exit vehicles to enter the building.

One of the men looks at his palm tablet. "It's been ruled accidental."

"How did it start?" asks another.

"Someone left a cig on their desk. It could have been smoldering all day." He puts his palm tablet back in his jacket. "We'll do a quick room-by-room check until the teks get here."

It takes a full hour for the four state teks to show up. Two males and two females, dressed haphazardly, and all looking like they just got out of bed. They carry their briefcases of equipment through the main entrance and up the stairs. The stationed police wave them through without checking IDs.

"How long will it take?" a policeman asks them.

"We should be done in thirty minutes or so," one of the teks answers.

"Good."

The state's data security director waits for them at the top of the stairs on the third floor. "I heard what you said, but I need you to be thorough or we'll all be here a lot longer than thirty minutes. All the fire damage was confined to the second-floor offices, but we need to know if anything was accessed at all on our floor."

"We know our jobs, sir," the lead tek says, irritated. He turns to his teks and says, "You two new guys take the back-up room. We'll take main security."

They brush past the director. One male/female team goes down one hallway; the other team goes down the other.

The lead and his female tek are done with their checks. "I'll check on the other two. You shut down here."

"Okay," she answers.

He exits the main security room with its bank of vid-screen

monitors and display consoles.

"What's the word?" asks the data director.

"All clear on our end. I'm checking the other team."

"Good. I want to get the hell out of here."

The back-up room is at the farthest end of the third floor. Its entrance is hidden by a secret, biometric-enabled door made to look like part of the wall. It opens as he nears.

He sees them and stops. "What are you doing?" he asks, watching the two teks type on the virtual keyboards of the secure consoles in the small room.

"We're testing an algorithm," the male tek says.

"Are the checks done?"

"Yes, we did that in the first two seconds here."

"Then what are you doing now?"

"Do you always ask questions to people who are not even here?" the man asks.

It takes a full hour for the two state teks to show up. One male and one female, dressed haphazardly, and both looking like they just got out of bed. They carry their briefcases of equipment through the main entrance and up the stairs. The stationed police wave them through without checking IDs.

"How long will it take?" a policeman asks.

"We'll be done in thirty minutes," the lead tek answers.

"Good."

The state's data security director waits for them at the top of the stairs on the third floor. "I heard what you said, but I need you to be thorough or we'll all be here a lot longer than thirty minutes. All the fire damage was confined to the second-floor offices, but we need to know if anything was accessed at all on our floor."

"We know our jobs, sir," the lead tek says, irritated. He turns and says, "You two new guys take the back-up room. We'll take main security." He stops in place.

"Two new guys?" the female tek asks. "What are you talking about? You're still in a drug daze, aren't you?"

"There were four of us before…there are two of us now."

He looks at his tek and the data director then bolts past them up the stairs and to the back-up room. It opens and he runs in. The female tek and the director are right behind him.

"They were here. They were accessing something at that console there." He points.

"What do you mean?" the director asks. "Who? What are you talking about?"

"I feel…sick." The lead tek loses his balance and falls to the floor.

Trog-land, Arkansas
12:14 a.m., 4 February 2096

The two Magi, Wings and Top Hat, do not say a word as they are led into the dark and dirty room by two large, grungy men. Inside, the crime boss sits at his desk with a big smile. Six henchmen stand behind him. Wings places a glowing white cube in front of him on the table.

The crime boss leans forward in his chair, his head coming within inches of the glowing cube. He continues smiling as his men crowd around it.

"Is that it?" one of the henchmen asks.

"Let me touch it," another henchman says.

As he does, a surge of immense energy rips through his body. The man screams as he is thrown back, knocking the boss and all of the men violently into the wall. His body wildly flops across the floor, intensifying in luminescence.

"Hold him down. He's destroying my place!" the boss yells.

The Magi stand where they are, without emotion.

"I got him!" One of the henchmen jumps on the man, and the other six pile on top.

A wave of electric energy ripples through all of them. It is now a mass of glowing and flopping bodies across the floor of the room. One of them knocks over the table and the white cube falls to the ground. *The room explodes!*

The bloodied and bruised boss picks himself off the ground. There is nothing left of his room but ashes and rubble. The building itself was only a simple shack. The two Magi stand watching him, not a mark on them, as if nothing happened. The boss looks around for his men, but sees none of them. He notices a glow from underneath the debris.

"What happened to my men?" he asks.

"I believe the phrase is 'spontaneous combustion by external means,'" Wings answers.

The boss can't stop smiling. "How do I pick up the cube?"

"Use fabric. Static energy is okay, but kinetic and thermal can be a problem."

The boss stands and rips a piece of fabric from his tattered top. He kicks the debris away and uses the fabric to pick up the cube carefully.

"There is no power cube on the market anywhere as powerful as this." He looks up at them. "You said you didn't want money?"

"Information."

"I'll give you any information you want. Name it."

"Do the Sons of Anarchists still view the Grid government as their enemy?"

"Of course we do. The Grid is order. We are chaos."

"Then we'll show you how to take down the state's Grid."

"Why? Is the Jew-Christian Revolution beginning again? I can get all Anarchists, Nihilists, and Hedonists to join us."

"No revolution, just a little chaos to satisfy certain shared anarchistic impulses."

The crime boss stares at the power cube. "Whatever you need. I don't think any part of the Grid has ever gone dark, at least not since fusion power went online, way back when. I don't think they would even know what to do." He laughs. "They'll reconnect it quickly though."

"That's okay. The point will be made."

"Then let's shut it down and watch the tek-dwellers live in some fear and darkness for a while." He holds the cube in the air. "With this, I'll be able to create my own anarchist city in the Troglands. We'll never need to secretly suck power from the Grid again."

"The first true Anarchist city in all of America with you as its ruler, its president," Wings says.

"President? Yeah, my own government. My government free of the Grid!"

Chapter Six: The Keeper

It's the only robot she has ever had, an old, foot-high, battery-powered maintenance bot that's been in a drawer all these years. She had it working all night to clean out the dust, dirt, and anything else it could find under there.

She gives a heavy sigh before she starts. To snake through the underfloor crawlspace, fighting her claustrophobia and fear of crawly things—spiders, roaches, and rats—will take who knows how long. Whenever she hears others walking outside, she stops and turns off the light on her headband lamp. She has been crawling in the cramped space for nearly an hour before she sees the opening. The sounds of her neighbors are gone and she continues. She reaches the opening and gets on all fours to crawl for another few feet before she can stand.

The mystery remains. *What shut off all power for the city?* It happened last night with no warning. From her hidden basement-level home, she could hear people scream and run around in panic. The the power was reactivated within no more than five minutes—but not for her. She isn't an official resident of the living complex.

She's an off-Grid squatter, hiding and unknown to all, secretly siphoning power from the Grid as she has done for the last five years. No one knows she is here and that is why she is alive. The American government would put her in a box, never see the light of day again, for her treason. Every other government, especially the CHINs, would put her in a box to extract all her 'god knowledge,'—her knowledge of creating synthetic, biological life-forms. And then there were the Jew-Christians, who would simply make her disappear for her 'atrocities'—creating her Children, the Hell Boys, the Man Made Out of String, and many, many other things.

But I am smarter than all of them combined.

Unfortunately, she has to manually re-enable the leech-link she set up when she first settled into her self-imposed prison-home. Infrastructure engineering is one of her many proficiencies. There are whole regions of people who want to live off-Grid—unconnected to the surveillance and control of the Grid government. She wonders how many others like her are simply hiding within tek-cities themselves, living an entire existence within the Grid, but still off-Grid.

The work is done. She starts her long crawl back, listening for any sound along the way. Every time she hears walking, speaking, or running, she stops. There are more than five thousand people living in the apartment tower above her, not including their pets, both organic and robotic. Like any other residential tower in a tek-city, the little power she uses off the Grid is too negligible to be detected. No one knows she's here, which is what will keep her safe and allow her to live a long life, despite an army of hunters.

The light from her headlamp appears first as she finally emerges from the other end of the crawlspace. Almost ninety minutes this time to get back. She had to stop several times along the way, nearly three hours in total, to complete her task. She stands and pushes the heavy door open very, very slowly. Once through, she closes it. Now she begins her walk through a small maze of hallways until she reaches the one secret door enabled by an old analog locking mechanism. Doors today don't even have doorknobs or locks. That's what biometric tek is for, but here she needed something nonelectrical, quiet, simple, and effective for her needs. She walks through and closes the door behind her. It is but one of five different doors she has to unlock by means of a combination lock—every door has a different code.

She passes through the last door and gives a mental sigh of relief as she closes it behind her. Home sweet home! She chain links the door in three places, lifts and places two different steel bars to barricade the door, and steps back to put a steel rod at an angle to further secure the door. There are no other entrances to her secret, underground, five-room home.

Having not been outside its doors in five years, she instinctively checks every closet, every cupboard, everything, and finally looks under her bed. She doesn't expect to find anyone, but it satisfies her internal voice—her paranoia.

"Did you miss me?" She plops down on the old couch in the living room. "That's the longest we've been apart from each other. What did you do while I was gone?"

She already knew about the effects of prolonged isolation before she made her run from the Zoo. So many try to fight it or ignore it. She embraced it. Knowing she would suffer ill effects, she created her own companions right from the start—her new Children. Floppy and Lovie were her two flexible mannequins— her surrogate daughter and son in unisex clothing. Her daughter, Lovie, with her female mannequin head and white clothes, is situated on the main living room couch. Her son, Floppy, in black clothes, is on one of the stools in the dining-kitchen room.

"I'm so tired. I told you two to make your mother do more exercise. Time for a nap."

The Keeper gets up from her couch and walks to her bedroom. She throws herself on top of the single bed. Her eyes are already closed and a deep sleep soon follows.

I am not smarter!

Her eyes pop open as quickly as she awakens.

Why did the Grid go down? The Grid has never gone down. Never in my entire life. Why now? Why this state?

She sits up in the bed.

No, I'm paranoid. They wouldn't shut down the power of a state to find me. They would, but they couldn't find me that way. How would they know which state? I'm not using enough power to be noticeable to anyone.

She starts to lie down again, then sits back up.

But a machine could be programmed to notice it. A machine could detect even the most infinitesimal level. My leech-link!

She jumps up from the bed, but stops.

But I would have to leave my home again. Crawl all the way there and back again. Then what would I do? I would have no power. No power, no lights. I could use just candles, but I don't have enough. And I don't have enough matches to cook with real fire. I'm not set up to cook with real fire. I couldn't tap into the Net. Could I take baths with cold water? Can I live without power? Human beings did so in the past. Human beings of the past were Neanderthals. I'm a woman of the soon-to-be twenty-second century. Humans of the past could find food, kill it, skin it, cook it—survive. Without canned food, I'd be dead. They could make a meal of a rat. I'd rather die.

She sits down on the floor, panicking.

What do I do?

"Children, what do I do?" She looks at them.

Should I go back out? Disconnect the link? Or am I being paranoid? No, I'm being paranoid. No one can find me. It's all in my mind. They can't find me. None of them can. There must be thousands of people illegally leeching. There must be people leeching right here. How would they know it's me? They couldn't. I barely use any power at all. Nothing that could be noticed by even a machine.

The Keeper smiles to herself and stands back up.

"Children, your mother is giving herself a panic attack for no reason. If anyone comes anywhere near us, I'll vaporize them. We have all the weapons we need to protect ourselves. Isn't that right, children?"

She walks to the refrigerator, opens it, and takes a collapsible tek-rifle from the door. She extends it open.

"Maybe I should carry this around until I feel safe again, children. Any change to our routine can bring on these feelings. We were fine for five years until last night. It could be a coincidence, but we must be cautious anyway."

She looks at Lovie.

"You're right. I can't shoot a weapon in here. The neighbors will hear. Who knows what Grid sensors could be outside? Yes, they could pick up even the faintest weapon discharge." She points to them. "But this tek-gun here, I almost forgot, I modified it for silent mode. I modified them all. They shoot energy discharges with no noise at all. See this modified muzzle? It's ready for firing."

She places the tek-rifle on the living room table, then returns to the refrigerator. She searches through the door and the food bins for additional weapons, including stun and sonic grenades. The only food in the refrigerator is on the corner of the top shelf. She loads up her arms and walks to the dining room table—where she sits most of the time—to dump the weapons there. After almost half an hour of talking to her children and herself, she has the weapons arranged on the table just as she wants.

"I feel comfortable now." She looks at her children again. "My paranoia will pass in a few days or so and then everything will go back to normal. I'll stay off Net and push back my normal weekly search-and-play sessions for maybe a week or two. Whatever news is happening in the world will wait. And our upstairs neighbors are all so noisy. We can tell everything we need to know by listening to them walk around. That's our best indicator of trouble. If their routine changes, we know something is wrong, but their routine never changes."

Routine. I haven't eaten yet.

"I say that and I'm not following my own routine. You both must be calling me a hypocrite. What canned delight should we have today for breakfast?"

She walks back into the kitchen and opens one of the cupboards—every inch of the four shelves is filled with silver cans. She grabs one and reads.

"What do you think of seafood today? I'm feeling for something meatier, though. What do you think?"

She looks at them and freezes. Her smile is gone from her face. She turns her head back to the can. It is a simple silver can, but she spends minutes examining it as her eyes tear up slightly.

She puts the can back in the cupboard, closes it, and opens another filled with bottles of alcohol. A blue bottle at the back is the one she grabs. She opens another cupboard and takes out a glass and a bottle opener. Using the tool, she carelessly opens the bottle, breaking the cork, and fills the glass with the bluish narco-alcohol. She plants herself on the single living room couch and drinks from the glass with one hand, pouring more from the bottle with the other.

She doesn't even notice it happen, but the entire room becomes dark except for where she is sitting. Floppy is not in his normal black unisex clothes; his clothes are white. She can see only his legs and white slip-on shoes. She looks again at Lovie. Her legs are dressed in black, with black heeled shoes. She can't see her clearly above the waist, but the top hat is unmistakable.

The Keeper sits quietly, holding both her glass and a nearly empty bottle.

"I hate you both. We were happy here and you've spoiled it."

She looks at Wings in the larger living room couch in the corner, his eyes glowing red. Top Hat watches her from the dining room stool, her eyes also glowing red and her teeth glowing white, showing a wide smile.

"Get out of my home!" she yells.

"You are getting used to living down below," Wings says. "As with all evil people."

"Down below? Is that some Jew-Christian reference? I am not an evil person!" She can feel hysteria growing within her—the feeling of being utterly trapped; the feeling of having her sanctuary violated. "I am atoning for everything I did. That's why I live here. It's my prison and I haven't left for five years. And before I came here, I destroyed the Zoo and all its subjects. That's what I did, not you. I am a good person."

She looks up. Top Hat's head with its glowing eyes is spinning around in one hundred-eighty-degree circles.

"I am not an evil person."

The Keeper is startled. Wings is somehow sitting across from her on something, maybe the air itself. She stares at him.

"You have no right to do this," she says. "Look at all the books I have on my tablets—goodness, morality, kindness, altruism. I cannot be blamed for being born and raised in amorality, but I have taught myself to transcend who I was. I should be praised for what I've accomplished, not hunted. What gives you the right to do this?"

"Excuse me," Wings interrupts. "I think there has been a misunderstanding. Do you believe we are here to harm you for your previous actions? We are only here to relay some information to you. Your current living choices are not our concern."

"You did all this, broke into my home, by impossible means to…to relay some information to me? That's it?"

"Yes."

"What information?"

"One of your daughters was killed in an accident, and we thought a furlough from your self-imposed prison sentence was in order for you to pay your last respects."

She watches him, then glances at his companion. "I am not leaving here, and none of your games will make me."

"But you've already left once."

"Because of you! You cut the power. I know it was you. I had no other choice." She tries to fight the impulse to ask the question, to not fall into their trap. She can't help herself. "I have no daughters!"

"We have obviously upset you and that was not our intention. We will leave you here in your solitude with your mannequin children to live out your life. None of the governments searching for you will ever find you. We'll just have to find another way into the Zoo."

"Zoo?"

"You didn't think that you'd destroy one Zoo and they would stop. They have created an impressive new one. It is larger than the old one by ten-fold. We needed your help to breach it, but we see now that such a reunion would be too psychologically disturbing for you. Fighting one's insectophobia or claustrophobia is one thing, but clone-ophobia is on another level of fear that we were wrong in thinking you'd be able to handle."

"What are you talking about? If there's another Zoo, then that's not my fault."

"It is. Your sisters run it."

"I have no sisters!"

"Your sister-daughters." Wings smiles and points to her lap. The Keeper jumps in her chair. A tablet is on her lap.

"You're like evil magicians tormenting me. I'm not touching it." She jerks her body to throw the tablet to the ground.

The tablet levitates with the display on. The Keeper immediately sees it and leans forward.

"Oh no!"

She grabs the tablet from the air. After staring at it, cursing under her breath, she throws it across the room. Quietly she sits with her eyes closed for the longest time. She opens them. Wings and Top Hat are sitting together now, slightly hidden in the darkness of the dimly lit room.

"How many sister-daughters do I have?"

"With the untimely death of one…one hundred," Wings answers.

The Keeper can barely contain her rage and jumps up from her chair. She clenches her fists against her temple and yells out. She summons every ounce of her self-control to speak in a tone less than a yell. "I had a colleague once who came up with the term 'clone-rape.' She was so paranoid about not letting her genetic material get into the hands of anyone. 'Leave it to scientists to come up with a unique way to rape a woman,' she would say. How did they get my genetic material? I was so careful. I destroyed everything. I left nothing behind—not a fingerprint, hair sample, skin flake. Nothing was left behind."

"How long is your…prison term?" Wings asks. The Keeper notices that the female never speaks.

"I have five years to go."

"Seems rather short."

"Ten years of solitary confinement is not short. I will probably have deep socialization problems for the rest of my life. Tell me what game you're trying to pull me into. I don't believe you when you say you're not here to kill me. Tell me what you came here for."

"Visit the Zoo."

"And do what?"

"You decide. You'll be reunited with your…family. You decide what course of action should be taken."

"They are not my family! Are you convinced that I will come to the same conclusion as you?"

"Only the reunion with your sister-daughters will answer the question for you."

"I'm tired. I thought I had gotten away. I was going to serve my prison term and then try to live a quiet life, but you won't let me. Reunion with my sister-daughters? Clones illegally made from me, without consent! Another Zoo. I can't take all this. I want it to end. I lived without all this for five years. I was content here, talking to myself and my children. I wasn't bothering anyone. Why couldn't you leave me alone? Let someone else do it. You do it. You destroy the new Zoo. You don't need me. You're intelligent. You can walk through walls and levitate things. Why me?"

"You can do something we can't"

"What? What can insignificant me do?"

"You aren't insignificant because your work isn't insignificant. We are all what we do. It is your legacy that has obsessed you these past years. What you can do that we can't is simply walk into the Zoo, through all its security measures, enter any secure area, access any system, and do anything you want. You won't be the one called the Keeper, the fugitive, the traitor, the evil monster maker. You'll be just one of a hundred clone-sisters doing their routine work in the wonderful Zoo. In the end, you will decide what your legacy will be. You all have the same face. Will the world know you by your work…or theirs?"

"It's not my fault. I'm not responsible for them."

"In theological tenets, every man or woman has free will. You are free to do what you will, but you must be free to accept the consequences that result—all of them. 'For every action, there will be a reaction.' That's a universal scientific tenet. You are the creator of your own misery, so only you can be the creator of its end."

The Keeper sits there, crying.

Chapter Seven: The Zoo

Trog-land Territory, Arkansas
2:11 a.m., 7 February 2096

An almost endless patchwork of buildings, shacks, tents, vans, RVs, and trucks makes up the city. And this Trog-land city is at war. A steady stream of flares illuminates the nighttime sky to reveal attack drones and approaching aircraft. The government drones fire at anything moving on the ground among the residents of the city. Anarchist, Nihilist, Hedonist, and Goth mobs fire back with their hand weapons. One of the crafts lands and its rear door opens, Armed robot shock troops run out to take positions against the residents.

"We have to cease fire," the Anarchist leader says.

"What! Why?" yells one of his fellow Anarchists. "The Grid government is invading. We kill them all."

"I have a plan. This isn't part of the plan. Why won't anyone listen? We can have the first Anarchist city in the world with our own Anarchist government and I have the means to power it without the Grid for centuries."

"Anarchist government?" another asks.

"Yes."

The other Anarchist shoots the Anarchist leader in the head, and he drops dead.

"There is no such thing as an *Anarchist government*! Chaos all the time and only the strongest survive. Now I am the leader of the clan. That's how it works."

Another Anarchist shoots the new leader in the face, and he also falls dead. "No, I want to be the clan leader. And why didn't you kill him *after* we got the power cube? Now what? The clan will waste days trying to find it."

"Here they come!" another Anarchist yells.

The robots break through their barricades and open fire. Some of the Anarchists are cut down by pulse blasts. Others duck or dive for cover, while others run away. Another runs at the robots and blows several apart with tek-rifle fire.

"It's World War Me!" he yells, laughing.

"Me?" one of his clan yells at him.

"The name of this city!" He laughs, raising his tek-rifle in the air in defiance. He is shot dead by approaching robots.

More Anarchists arrive and the gun-battle intensifies.

Two of the robot surrogates break away from the main attack formation and walk to the farthest end of the Trog-town. The gunfire in the distance is accompanied by repeated explosions. The robots reach their destination and stop. Their legs drill through the ground and it glows as they get closer. The robots morph into their true selves. Wings picks up the cube and puts it into his jacket as giant white wings rise from his back. A pair of black wings rises from Top Hat's back. The couple doesn't fly, but floats up from the ground into the night sky and disappears.

Monster Island, Indian Ocean
9 a.m., 7 February 2096

The hover-jet sets down on the island's landing field. Mary waits, standing next to a little brown-haired girl of no more than three years old. Three bald, bearded, and muscular guards stand behind them. Niccolo exits and approaches on the dirt path.

"My heart always smiles when family is reunited," Niccolo says. A look of disgust comes over Mary's face. "Hello, Linda."

"Hi," the little girl answers.

Mary says nothing as Linda glances at her.

"This, dear doctor, is the end," he says to Mary. "We will probably never lay eyes on each other ever again. News that I know is as welcome to your ears as it is to mine." He pauses for some kind of response, but gets none. "You have full control of the facility, the island's surveillance network, all security androids, and all maintenance bots. You and your daughter will both have the control access codes.

"The island's defense systems have been augmented, though. If you make any attempt to leave the island without your work being complete, all defense barriers will immediately shut down and all the hellish life-forms will be able to go anywhere and hunt you both down. Do you know what happens then, Linda?"

"They'll eat us," she says.

"Good, you understand. You seem to understand all this much better than your mother."

"You must be proud. Scaring a little girl," Mary says.

"The only thing she should be scared of is you," Niccolo says. "She'll come to know how much of a selfish animal you really are."

Mary ignores him. She wants to say something but doesn't.

He continues, "If you're feeling especially daring and think you can outrun all of them or think you can outsmart them, you should know that the water will be crawling with them too. If you think you can swim past them and get to the outer perimeter, you will be able to celebrate…for a few seconds. None of the organisms can be allowed to escape into the general ecosystem, so anything reaching the outer perimeter will activate the final fail-safe."

Mary says, "You rigged the island? What kind of bomb?"

"Your bodies won't be able to distinguish the type of blast, so what should it matter?"

"Why are you going through all of this? Why not destroy the island, kill all the creatures, and kill me now? Why this game?"

Linda looks at her. "I think it'll be fun. It's better than playing vid-games. That's fake. This is real fun. It'll be fun, Mary."

"They're using us," she snaps.

"I know that. But it'll still be fun."

"You didn't answer my question, Mr. Niccolo. Why don't you just end this now? You hate us. Why trust me with this? Stop the games and end it now."

"You'll figure it out one day…if you live long enough."

"We kill all the creatures in your game and we get to go free?" Mary asks again.

"When the island is cleared of all its unnatural life-forms, the system will give you all the exit codes, and an automated helicopter will arrive and set down for you. You can use the system library to read up on how to fly one."

"How long will it take for us to clear the island?" Linda asks.

"That is up to you. It could be five years, ten years, or twenty years. It is all in your hands."

Mary is visibly angry again. Linda glances at her, then back at Niccolo.

"Have a nice life, both of you."

"Bye, bye," little Linda says.

Niccolo manages a last smile. He turns and walks back down the dirt path. The three White guardsmen follow. Mary and Linda watch them until they reach the hover-jet, climb aboard, and close the doors. The aircraft begins its vertical ascent. It hovers at twenty feet above the ground and flies away.

In the distance, they can hear all the howls, barks, growls, bird calls, and unrecognizable animal sounds of the island.

"Why are we here?" Mary asks aloud. "What are their real motives in having us do this?"

"Who cares?" Little Linda says. "Let's just kill monsters."

Over the Indian Ocean
9:27 a.m., 7 February 2096

Niccolo smiles as he watches Mona Lisa speak to him from the secure vid-screen.

"We're done," Mona Lisa says.

Niccolo nods.

"Were the profilers correct?" she asks.

"Yes," Niccolo answers. "The daughter is exactly what we wanted. More than what we had hoped."

"Our 'friend?'"

"She's on her way there to be *friendly* to our other 'friends.'"

"I wish we destroyed this monster island too. But I understand the Continuum's decision. We know they'll rebuild eventually, so let it be on our terms and on the road that we guide them to. I'm glad to be done with them, though."

"As am I."

"*Bueno.* See you back at New Vatican. It will be good to be home. Safe flight and God bless."

"You too. God bless."

The Zoo, One Hundred Miles East of the Fiji Islands
8 a.m., 9 February 2096

The Keeper manually drives her yellow car down the elevated roadway that hovers above the ocean. These roadway structures are very common among island territories and are used to connect multiple islands for car-bound travel. She is casually dressed in a simple white dress. A yellow scarf covers her hair and dark glasses are over her eyes. It is a beautiful fifty-nine-mile drive—cool breeze, and not another person or car around, in either direction. In these remote regions, there is no auto-drive, no drones, no urban sprawl; only the pure nature—or the facsimile of such—to get lost in. She can't help but be impressed. They created an entire island of unimaginable size.

As she nears the main island itself, she sees miles of nothing but desert terrain, in stark contrast to the green-covered islets she passed. RESTRICTED AREA signs in multiple languages come into view. Some would say it is odd that they would put such a critical facility near a busy, public, year-round travel destination. A little reverse psychology at work—"it couldn't be that restricted in an exotic place like this." She reaches the regular black asphalt road to the only visible structure.

All she had to do was drive into the facility—nothing more. A simple three-person guard shack at the perimeter of the man-made desert on a man-made island with nothing else as far as the eye could see. The gate sensors scanned her down to the DNA level and the robotic guards waved her in as the series of gates opened.

As she drives in, she notices that the road is under a camouflaged anti-satellite net. From the air or from space, it undoubtedly looks exactly like the surrounding desert terrain. A car entrance rises from the ground as the roadway itself descends at a gentle incline. She removes her yellow head scarf as she drives in.

The facility is an underground mini-city, every wall and floor a shiny white surface. The clear floor is a two-part, walkway with the left side moving in one direction and the right side moving in the opposite. All scientists and staff are dressed in white.

The Keeper walks through the main door dressed in a white lab coat, too. There are no physical guards; everything is automated. Sensors watch everyone at all times using every wavelength. The Keeper's biometrics are recognized and all the inner doors automatically open for her.

9:32 a.m.

She sits alone in a lab, typing on the virtual keyboard. The database vid-files flash across the inclined table display. At one point she stops and, disturbed, closes her eyes. She opens them and continues the review.

The door opens and someone enters. The Keeper stops to look up at the visitor. It is her, twenty years younger—*a clone of the Keeper.*

"Hello Mother," Ambrosia-41 says. The smiling clone walks right up to the desk. "I never in my life thought we'd actually ever meet. We thought you were dead. We're so glad you're not."

The door opens again and several more clones enter the lab. Each one walks to the desk. The Keeper now has eight grinning clones standing a foot in front of her.

"You are older than we are, Mother. Visibly older," Ambrosia-50 says.

"Mother, we never imagined you'd be foolish enough to try this. There are only one hundred of us left, but today there were one hundred and one registered on the counter. Why are you here, Mother?" Ambrosia-23 asks.

"Then the death of our sister was not an accident after all," Ambrosia-72 says. "We prepared for this, Mother, no matter how remote its possibility."

"And here I am." The Keeper takes her hands from the virtual keyboard. "I had to see what my genetic offspring were doing in my name." All the clones reach into lab jackets and pull out guns as she speaks. "I needed to know that you were good enough to carry on the family business."

"Mother, are you lying to us?" Ambrosia-25 asks. "The last time you were in a lab you did a lot of bad things. You killed Hitler, Stalin, and Mao. You killed all the 'animals.'"

The clones point their weapons at her. The Keeper smirks.

"What are you all doing? I come all this way to check your progress and this is how you greet me. My intention was to come and go without anyone knowing. Put the guns away."

The door opens and more clones stream into the room. For a moment she doesn't know how to react to seeing herself—multiple copies of herself, all sentient beings made from her genetic material. The clones cluster around the desk on both sides.

"Good. I won't have to repeat myself one hundred times."

"We are so happy to meet you, Mother," they all say together. The new clones also pull guns from their lab jackets.

"Don't do that. Talk all together. It's freakish. Now, I've been reviewing your work, but I need to directly see the subjects you've created."

"Are you going to try to kill them too, Mother?" Ambrosia-72 asks.

"How would I do that? You have the weapons. This facility has far better security than the original Zoo, though I'm disappointed that you would even allow me access." The Keeper stands from the desk. "I want to see these subjects. I'm not going to have you disgrace the Ambrosia genetic line."

"How have we done that, Mother?" Ambrosia-38 asks.

"Take me there now and I'll show you." The Keeper walks through her clone-daughters to the door. She stops and turns. "I am the genetic original, the clone-mother, so you listen to me. Take me there now. I don't have all day and I want to be out of here by the end of the day."

The grinning clones look at each other. They follow her out of the room.

"Tell us, Mother, do you think your plan is going to work?" Ambrosia-51 asks.

"What plan?" the Keeper asks. "There is no plan. Will this elevator take us there?"

"Yes, Mother. It will," they say.

The elevator opens and three more Ambrosia-clones are waiting. The Keeper smiles and says, "I'm everywhere."

"Welcome to the Menagerie, Mother," Ambrosia-2 says. "However, I must say that the myth of you was far more appealing than the reality of you. You were the one who got away, that made us proud of our Mother. Now you've returned and spoiled the myth."

"I would say that you are the genetic disgrace to the line, Mother," Ambrosia-11 says.

"Then what does that make you as my genetic copies? Is this all of you?" she asks.

"Yes, Mother. All of us are here," Ambrosia-1 says. "But your journey ends here and your plot will not even be allowed to be set in motion."

"Do I not even get to see the subjects?" the Keeper asks.

"No, you don't," Ambrosia-2 says. "We don't know what your

plan is, but we will not let you get any closer."

"So close, yet so far," the Keeper says, almost jokingly. "My sister-daughters are not unintelligent, only evil."

"We would have wanted to do at least a cursory psychological interview, Mother," Ambrosia-27 says. "To record your feelings about being surrounded by, in essence, yourself."

"Mother, there is no such thing as evil. It's all a matter of socialization according to norms of those in power," Ambrosia-2 says.

"I once believed it to be an arbitrary construct of the religious, until I saw differently. Good and evil transcend religiosity and irreligiosity."

"Mother, how did you get the nickname 'The Keeper'?" Ambrosia-27 asks.

"I created the Zoo. I created its most promising subjects. They were all my children. I created them, raised them, nurtured them. I was their Keeper. Then I was their executioner."

"Mother, does this story have an ending?"

"Strangely, I am glad that we had a chance to meet this one time."

The Keeper raises her left hand and a yellow pulse explodes from the palm. She is temporarily blinded by the flash.

All she hears are screams. She sees the orange glow through her eyelids. She can feel the intense heat as she opens her eyes. The clones are all ablaze, smoldering embers of ash that crumble to the ground.

The Keeper sits on the floor of the antechamber. She stares at the burned-out corpses of her sister-children. The pristine white hallway looks sick and putrid with the blackish-brown and reddish ash. They were going to kill her but she killed them first. She should have no feelings for them at all. They were unsanctioned creations of her, not sim-clones, but real clones. They should have never been 'born.' But they were.

The lights are all flashing red; the facility is on lock-down. She is now unable to get through the door she needs to enter, but no security measures on Earth will keep her out of the Zoo. She can see a long hallway to another door. She looks at her new android hand—it is flashing blue.

She stands from the floor. Doors don't have doorknobs anymore, but—*Let's see what else my new hand can do, courtesy of the Magi.* The Keeper punches the door once and surprises herself when it falls in.

The clear elevator descends to a large, man-made, dimly lit cavern. She stops the descent, as she doesn't need to go any farther. Floating in suspended animation inside clear bubbles are the creatures—the *subjects*. The bubbles are secured by massive rods from both the ceiling and floor of the cavern. Metallic cables are attached to the bubbles, equally spaced. They are to stimulate muscle tissue and maintain brain attentiveness even as the subjects hibernate. None of the creatures are smaller than twenty feet—a furry porcupinoid, a rocky-armored arachnoid, a metalloid-scaled reptilian, and something with bat-like wings. They all are curled up in fetal positions, so she can't clearly make out their features. She cannot see any other bubble-containers, but imagines that there are more, maybe many more. She touches the controls to move the elevator back up to the secure labs.

The hallway lights are flashing red and she runs. The walls alternate between transparent and solid, and she looks into each lab as she goes. She stops at one, seeing an active console, and pushes the door. It doesn't respond to her biometrics. She punches down the door with her left hand.

She types quickly to access the database from the console. She stops and looks up toward the door.

Did I see something?

She watches for a while. A silhouetted figure peeks into the room from the hallway. It knows it has been seen, so it enters.

It was impossible that a facility of this size would have only one hundred clones working in its labs. The man stops at the door, wearing a black uniform—a one-piece jumpsuit and a cap. There's something strange about him—his head is vibrating.

She fires from the palm of her left hand. The pulse hits his head dead-center. His head blows up in flames, but his body breaks apart and flies at her. The Keeper ducks as the robot's right arm just misses her. She fires again and hits one of the legs jumping to her. The chest crashes on the console and she dives for the floor. Laser pulses from the chest shatter the floor, but she fires again— once at the chest and again just as the robot's disembodied arm grabs her ankle. She clenches her teeth to stop herself from yelling out in pain. Her ankle is crushed, and she looks at her body to see that she's been hit at least once. She moves her body back to the wall in pain.

The other robot leg attacks, launching itself like a missile at her. All she can do is raise her left hand to block it. The robot piece is blown apart in flaming pieces.

So here is where I die. I spent all my time in Zoos and now I'll die in one, even though I tried to get away. I had gotten away for a time. I was going to live a good life.

An identical robot enters the room, followed by many others.

"This is more like it," she says, trying to laugh through the pain. "Make new types of organic life *and* new types of robots, too." The room is now filled with nearly two dozen robots. "Well, at least I'll be killed fast."

The facility's speaker system wails with proximity alarms— something is approaching. The robots run out of the room in formation.

The Keeper starts to laugh.

The facility descends into the ground as guard robots swarm out of exits, firing pulse lasers into the air. The sun's rays are blocked out as seemingly hundreds of thousands of missiles rain down from the sky. They hit the center of Zoo Island, exploding in one wave after another, destroying one level after another, and drilling and exploding through to its final cavern level.

A metallic orb falls from the sky, so large that it seems to be a quarter of the island's size. It crashes center-mass. The explosion makes almost no sound, and there is almost no blast cloud. The man-made island implodes on itself and there is nothing left. A complete void of space remains and then the ocean waters rush in. It is as if the Zoo was never there.

Science Division Building, Elizabeth Center, Anacostia, Southeast Washington, DC
6:02 a.m., 9 February 2096

Garrison's somber face stares back from the vid-screen. "Disappeared?" Garrison asks.

"Yes sir," a man's voice answers. "The event interfered with all EMP for a few seconds, but the range was thousands of miles away. We were able to calculate the epicenter. The island is gone."

"Blown up?"

"No, we have the sat-recon. Disappeared. Maybe they sunk it somehow. We now know the island was their largest facility in the world. We also know from all the chatter intercepts that they won't be able to reconstitute it. We're all watching this time."

Garrison nods.

"Seems like your plan is working, sir. These rogue elements are dropping like flies all over the world. The only place they may still be operating is Russian Bloc territory. Instructions, sir?"

"Get back here and let the locals handle the investigation. I need you to find any and all unaffiliated bio-scientists out there and hire them. All of them. I have the President's authorization. We can create endless dummy projects to keep them out of the hands of any independents—and our enemies for that matter—or keep them from becoming independents themselves. The President wants the entire independent bio-warfare market gone. Dry up the entire black market swamp once and for all."

"What about the Outlands and Trog-land territories? There are rumors of…creatures out there…and demons. Whatever that means."

"All of that is someone else's job. Homeland just had us on loan. It's back to creating life for us."

"Sir, I did bring this up before, but these Jew-Christians…they found their Monster Island, made it disappear. We don't have to make the independent bio-warfare market disappear; they already have. What is *their* end game?"

"*The* end game is whatever the President says it is."

"Not ours—"

"Yes, I know what you mean and my answer is still the same. Whatever the President says it is."

"Sir, I hope we're as smart as we think we are."

Garrison laughs. "We are. I'll keep repeating my mantra. Our mission is to protect the Homeland and our nation's interests with every scientific skill and know-how our division can achieve. But for us, it goes beyond that. We're charting a path for the continual advancement of the human race. There will be a day on this Earth when the mechanical and the biological will be one and the same—the new singularity of existence. I don't know what the word for this singularity of existence will be called then, but it will come to exist. Let's get back to making life. The brief era of these bio-punks is coming to an end."

Cyberspace, Continuum Meeting
11:57 p.m., 11 February 2096

Another secret, holographic, virtual meeting in Freespace concludes. A Faither leader closes.

"All of this was spurred by the strange murder of a Pagan reporter seven years ago. A strange assassin composed of a strange, sentient, biological matter and a stranger quantum robot. One pebble thrown into the water at one end—our enemies—and out came a tidal wave on the other—us. This assassin, incidentally, was the least important matter of this mission and the Magi have already located it. No, it was the Zoo, its creators, and the many, many smaller versions and islands they had built all over the world.

"I once had a dream similar to that old story of Rip Van Winkle. Instead of a pre-American Revolutionary War man sleeping through that war to find his children were grown adults and that there was a new world order, I woke up to the nightmare of an endless global war. Not among humans, as they had been destroyed many ages ago, but by their own slave creations. The endless war was between competing plagues of horrific robots and horrific creatures. The robots were self-replicating and the creatures had learned to clone themselves, both as determined to exterminate the other as they had done so successfully to humankind.

"We close Project Tek-Fall. We have accomplished all its goals, though we all know that the creators and creations that we destroyed are only precursors of what's to come. But then, we all know that people can be like angels in goodness, or the most horrible creatures of them all who never cease to do evil. Their mechanical and biological creations are a reflection of a fallen state, not the cause of it.

"And speaking of dreams of endless global wars and fallen men, the world's superpowers will be attending their first-ever summit hosted by the Russians in the Russian Bloc. The Presidents of America, the CHINs, and the Caliphate—all our enemies in one room. One can't help but wonder what chaos that little meeting will bring about.

"Project Noah is now our only project and must be completed as quickly as heavenly possible."

Twenty-nine years until the first attack of World War III. The After Eden Series continues in *Rising Leviathan (Book #3)*

REFERENCES

Goth Lila is in *Thy Kingdom Fall (After Eden Series, Book #1)* and *Stars and Scorpions (After Eden Series, Book #2)*.

M (a leader of the Protestant Christian Order) is in *Thy Kingdom Fall (After Eden Series, Book #1)* and *Stars and Scorpions (After Eden Series, Book #2)*.

Doctor Mary is introduced in *Stars and Scorpions (After Eden Series, Book #2)*, as is **Doctor Godwin**.

Mona Lisa is in *Stars and Scorpions (After Eden Series, Book #2)*.

Niccolo is in *Stars and Scorpions (After Eden Series, Book #2)*.

The Keeper is introduced in *Stars and Scorpions (After Eden Series, Book #2)*, as is a reference to **Klara**.

Sikh Bob is introduced in *Thy Kingdom Fall (After Eden Series, Book #1)*.

The mentioned **Tova** and **Mr. Tova** (leaders of the Conservative Jewish Order) are in *Stars and Scorpions (After Eden Series, Book #2)*.

The mentioned "General" **Moses** (leader of the Protestant Christian Order and husband of M) is in *Thy Kingdom Fall (After Eden Series, Book #1)*, *Stars and Scorpions (After Eden Series, Book #2)*, and *Rising Leviathan (After Eden Series, Book #3)*.

Gideon is a main protagonist in *Stars and Scorpions (After Eden Series, Book #2)*.

The **Jewish Wolf Pack** is in *Stars and Scorpions (After Eden Series, Book #2)*.

The mentioned **Father Marcos** is the other main protagonist in *Stars and Scorpions (After Eden Series, Book #2)*.

Archbishop Masai is in *Stars and Scorpions (After Eden Series, Book #2)*.

The **Magi** are in *Thy Kingdom Fall (After Eden Series, Book #1)*, *Rising Leviathan (After Eden Series, Book #3)* and *Red Halo (After Eden Series, Book #4)*.

President T. Wilson is in *Thy Kingdom Fall (After Eden Series, Book #1)* and *Rising Leviathan (After Eden Series, Book #3)*.

The Man Made Out of String is introduced in *Thy Kingdom Fall (After Eden Series, Book #1)*.

Project Noah is introduced in *Thy Kingdom Fall (After Eden Series, Book #1)*.

Project New People is introduced in *Stars and Scorpions (After Eden Series, Book #2)*.

The mentioned world summit is in *Rising Leviathan (After Eden Series, Book #3)*.

Thank you for reading!

Dear Reader,

I hope you enjoyed *Tek-Fall*.

<u>Can You Write Me a Review?</u>

If you enjoyed ***Tek-Fall* (An *After Eden* Companion Novel)**, I'd greatly appreciate a review on one or more of the following sites:

Reviews are the best way for readers to discover good books. My writer's motto is simple: "Readers Rule!" Thanks so much.

Always writing,

Austin Dragon

CONTINUE THE ADVENTURE

Get Your Next *After Eden* Book!

The After Eden Series (Chronological Order)

Thy Kingdom Fall (After Eden Series, Book #1)
Stars and Scorpions (After Eden Series, Book #2)
Metal Flesh (After Eden Series: Tek-Fall, Episode I)
Hell's Menagerie (After Eden Series: Tek-Fall, Episode II)
Rising Leviathan (After Eden Series, Book #3)
Pure Conspiracy (After Eden Select Novel)
Red Halo (After Eden Series, Book #4) Coming Soon!

The After Eden Series (Group Order)

Main After Eden Series
Thy Kingdom Fall (After Eden Series, Book #1)
Stars and Scorpions (After Eden Series, Book #2)
Rising Leviathan (After Eden Series, Book #3)
Red Halo (After Eden Series, Book #4) Coming Soon!

After Eden: Tek-Fall Companion Novels
Metal Flesh (After Eden Series: Tek-Fall, Episode I)
Hell's Menagerie (After Eden Series: Tek-Fall, Episode II)

After Eden Select Novel
Pure Conspiracy (After Eden Select Novel)

Also by Austin Dragon

See all my books in science fiction, cyberpunk, mystery, horror, YA dystopia, and fantasy at: **http://www.austindragon.com/books-of-author-austin-dragon/**

ABOUT THE AUTHOR

Austin Dragon is author of the *After Eden* **Series**, including the *After Eden: Tek-Fall* mini-series, the classic *Sleepy Hollow Horrors*, and the upcoming cyberpunk detective series, *Liquid Cool*. He is a native New Yorker, but has called Los Angeles, California home for the last twenty years. Words to describe him, in no particular order: U.S. Army; English teacher; one-time resident of Paris; political junkie; movie buff; campaign manager and staffer of presidential and gubernatorial campaigns; Fortune 500 corporate recruiter; renaissance man; dreamer.

He is currently working on the next books in the *After Eden* Series, and new books and series in mystery, fantasy, YA dystopia, classic horror, and more science fiction!

Connect with Austin on social media at:

Website and blog:

http://www.austindragon.com

Twitter:

https://twitter.com/Austin_Dragon

Pinterest:

http://www.pinterest.com/austindragon

Google+:

https://google.com/+AustinDragonAuthor

Goodreads:

https://www.goodreads.com/ADragon

www.ingramcontent.com/pod-product-compliance
Lightning Source LLC
Chambersburg PA
CBHW070448120726
47910CB00003B/972